Shandra Higheagle Mystery Books

Double Duplicity

Tarnished Remains

Deadly Aim

Murderous Secrets

Killer Descent

Reservation Revenge

Yuletide Slaying

Fatal Fall

Haunting Corpse

Artful Murder

Dangerous Dance

Shandra Higheagle Mystery

Paty Jager

Windtree Press

Hillsboro, Or

DANGEROUS DANCE

Contact Information: info@windtreepress.com

Windtree Press
Hillsboro, Oregon
http://windtreepress.com

Cover Art by Christina Keerins

Published in the United States of America

ISBN 9781943601899

Disclaimer

While I have a reader who lives on the Colville Reservation, she is not familiar with the Seven Drums Religion. I gathered the information I could from websites and the book, *A Little Bit of Wisdom: Conversations with a Nez Perce Elder* by Horace Axtell and Margo Aragon. I used creative license in the dance scenes, using bits and pieces of information I'd gathered from other books on Native American dance but followed the information in the Axtell book as much as possible for the Sunday Service.

Chapter One

The metal sculpture of the root diggers heralded
Shandra Higheagle's return to the Colville Reservation.
It had been months since she'd visited her family.
However, Aunt Jo had been on the phone with her
every week as they planned Shandra and Ryan's
wedding. She smiled. Less than a month the wedding
would be, here on the reservation, with his family and
hers present.

Shandra was excited about the doeskin wedding
dress her cousin was making. There were many things
she had to do and learn while she visited this week.
Aunt Jo had agreed to help her incorporate Nez Perce
traditions into their wedding day.

She glanced over at the Community Center and the
Powwow grounds beyond when she entered the
Agency. Aunt Jo had suggested she have the wedding
inside the center if the weather were bad and out on the
Powwow grounds if the weather allowed. Shandra was
torn. She'd envisioned the wedding being held at the

Higheagle Ranch.

Her heart warmed remembering how easily Ryan had agreed to all the Nez Perce traditions. However, he told her since she was marrying in clothing from her roots, he would be wearing cowboy boots, jeans, and a western cut jacket. Even though his family was Catholic, his mother was so happy he was finally getting married, she didn't mind that the ceremony wasn't being held in her church.

Shandra continued up the highway and into Nespelem. The small reservation town had become her second home since reuniting with her Nez Perce family three years earlier.

"If only I had known all these wonderful people while growing up." Passing her Aunt Velma's house, she wasn't surprised to see half a dozen cars parked in the driveway and the street. The woman seemed to always be advocating for something in Nespelem.

When they had worked as a team to prove Coop, her cousin, was innocent of a murder, Shandra and her aunt had become closer. If there hadn't been extra cars, she would have pulled in and given the woman a hug.

The drive along the Nespelem River to the Higheagle Ranch was green and lush. Wildflowers danced in the slight breeze, adding their yellow, purple, and orange to the landscape. The May weather was pleasant. Nothing like the harsh summer heat that would soon suffocate the area.

A bouquet of wildflowers would be pretty for her to carry in the wedding but by mid-June they would be hard to find. She'd ask Andy, Coop's brother, if there was a chance they could find some then.

She turned down the lane to the ranch and a feeling

of homecoming overcame her. Even though she couldn't remember the ranch before her mother took her away from the Higheagles at age four, when she'd made a visit as a teenager, and then as an adult, it had felt like home. Just as her ranch on Huckleberry Mountain had felt right when she'd set foot on it.

Aunt Jo stood among her chickens, casting grain about the ground. She glanced up and smiled. Dumping the remaining feed in a trough, she exited the chicken pen.

Shandra parked beside her uncle's pickup and grabbed her bag out of the back of the Jeep.

Her aunt met her half way to the house, hugging her.

"It's good to see you. And with such happy times ahead." Aunt Jo entered the house, holding the door open.

Shandra nodded. "I'm so happy everyone agreed to have my wedding on the reservation. I want all my family to be at the event."

"It is generous of you to want everyone." Aunt Jo wrinkled her nose. "There are a few you would be wise to not invite."

Shandra laughed. As with every family there was always a black sheep or two. "I sent out invitations to the important people," she nodded to the invitation she spied under a magnet on the refrigerator, "and an open verbal one to those who did not receive a paper invitation."

"You have two hours before Velma brings you the applications from the young women who applied for your generous scholarship." The pride in Aunt Jo's voice put a lump in Shandra's throat.

She'd come up with the scholarship idea while talking with people during her search to prove her cousin's innocence. With the help of other artists she knew, they'd put together an ongoing non-profit scholarship for young women who received a high school or general education diploma and wished to continue their education at college. She, Jo, and Velma made up the committee who chose the recipient. There would be one a year. She would have liked to give more but until she brought in more sponsors and profits from her sales, only one was feasible.

"I saw there were a lot of cars at Velma's when I came by. What group is meeting there today?" Shandra set her bag by the stairs to the rooms above and sat down behind a glass of iced tea her aunt had placed on the kitchen table.

"I can't keep up with her organizations. But she is tickled you are having the wedding here. She's offered to house Ryan's parents for the weekend of the wedding." Aunt Jo had her back to the table as she retrieved something from the counter.

Shandra wasn't sure Ryan's parents would be comfortable at Velma's house. Or any house on the reservation. They were open-minded country people. While they had a fair-sized family and didn't mind sticking their noses into their children's lives, they preferred to keep their family private.

"I believe Ryan reserved rooms for them at the Columbia River Inn. His whole family will be staying there." She hoped it wouldn't hurt her aunt's feelings.

Jo nodded. "Good. Everyone will be more comfortable that way."

Shandra grinned. Her family was generous to a

fault. They had offered. That the Greers had already taken care of their accommodations simplified matters. No one's pride would be hurt.

They sat at the table discussing the items that needed to be accomplished this week. Shandra's head was spinning with all the places Aunt Jo had planned for her to be while she was here. It seemed like more meetings, instruction, and planning than there would be time for in five days. She'd just written down the schedule when Velma walked through the back door carrying a folder.

"It's good to see you." Shandra stood, giving her aunt a hug.

The tall, broad woman blushed. "It's been quiet around here."

Jo retrieved another glass of iced tea and replenished Shandra's glass. "It looks like you received more applications since the last time we talked."

"We have fifteen to go through." Velma eased her large body onto a chair and picked up the tea. "It's starting to warm up. You might want Wendy to make you a bikini instead of a dress out of the doeskin. *Ays?*" her aunt joked, using the tagged-on Colville word, *ays*, that emphasized the joke.

"I'm so happy Wendy agreed to make me a traditional dress for the wedding. The work she showed me the last time I was here…It will be a prized possession and displayed in my house as a work of art."

Velma blushed, again, but pride shown in her eyes. "My Wendy learned to tan hides from my grandmother. She would spend the weekends with her learning the old ways of making clothing."

"It is a lost art. I'm so pleased she is teaching

classes at the college in Spokane." Shandra had asked an art professor she knew at the community college to contact her cousin about doing an adult ed class on tanning hides. Now Wendy was also slated to teach one on beading.

Shandra reached over and grabbed the folder from Velma, excited to read about the applicants.

"I've already picked out three that I think are deserving," Velma said. "They're on top."

Shandra read the names. Jenny Wells, Lauren Minto, and Pim Solomon. Of the three, she liked Pim. She'd taken five years to complete high school but only because she'd had to drop out for one year to help with her family when her mother was ill. That took dedication to return to school and get her high school diploma. She read each one and handed it over to Aunt Jo. At the very bottom, as if Velma had wanted to hide the application, was one for Nelly Bingham.

Starring at the name, Shandra's heart soared. This was the young woman who had given her the idea for the scholarship. A teenage pregnancy had caused her to drop out of school. Shandra had seen potential and told Nelly if she got her GED she could apply for the scholarship. She placed Nelly's application with Pim's.

Aunt Jo pulled another application out of the batch Shandra had passed along to her. Tammy Randal.

Shandra glanced at her aunt. "Really? A Randal?" She would never forget the viciousness of the Randal family when they believed Coop had killed Arthur Randal.

Jo shrugged. "She does come from a troubled background. She's a Randal."

Velma snorted.

Shandra laughed. "That's true." She tapped Nelly's application. "This is the reason I started the scholarship. I feel it's only right she is the first recipient."

Velma pursed her lips. She'd shown her disapproval of the young woman before.

Aunt Jo sighed. "She does deserve a second chance. We all know her grandmother won't be able to help her do better than sleeping around and waitressing at the bar."

"What about a runner-up in case Nelly doesn't accept?" Velma asked.

"Why wouldn't she accept?" Shandra peered at her aunt. "Do you know something?"

"Nothing that's fact."

"A vision?" Shandra asked. Velma belonged to the Seven Drum Society Shandra's grandmother had presided over before her death. They were also called the dreamer religion. The religion was starting to make a comeback with the Nez Perce after the religious orders who invaded their country pressured them to believe in Christianity rather than believing all creatures had power and were on earth before man.

"More a premonition."

Hoping her aunt was wrong, Shandra tapped Pim Solomon. "She can be the runner-up and can apply again next year."

Velma scooped all the papers back into the folder with the three applications they'd picked on the top. "When do we announce this?"

"Since we'll be at the community center tomorrow for my dancing instructions, why don't you call Nelly and ask her to come to the center at one. That will give me time to print out a certificate." Shandra was excited to see Nelly again and learn how the young woman was doing.

Chapter Two

The following day, Shandra rode to the community center with Aunt Jo. While her aunt dealt with matters pertaining to her job as the coordinator of the center, Shandra printed out a certificate and put together the scholarship packet she would give to Nelly at one.

Shandra pulled the video of Aunt Jo and Uncle Martin's wedding out of her purse and went in search of a television with a VHS player. Walking by the main entrance of the building, she glanced out the large windows to the parking lot.

A tall young man with a striking profile and long hair blowing in the wind was deep in discussion with a young woman who's back was to the building. It was evident neither one was happy with the conversation. The woman's arms were crossed, her body stiff. The man shoved his hair off his face, revealing a scowl and downturned mouth.

The two parted. The young man climbed into a jacked-up pickup and the young woman walked toward the road.

Shandra continued on her hunt for a VHS player, but her mind was on the couple. There had been something familiar about the young woman. Was it someone she'd met on the reservation before?

"What are you doing wandering around?" Aunt Jo asked.

"I was looking for a device to play this on." She glanced over her shoulder at the entrance. "I witnessed an argument between a young man and woman." She shook her head. "It was nothing. Where can I watch your wedding video?"

Aunt Jo smiled. "Right this way."

They entered a small room with a television unit that had a VHS player in its base.

Jo sat down beside her, and they watched the video together with Shandra asking questions about each action and spoken word.

"That was lovely!" she exclaimed, staring at her aunt. "You were beautiful then and still are."

"Thank you for the kind words, but I was a bride. All brides are beautiful because they are joining with their soul mate on their wedding day." She sighed. "To be that sure of anything else in my life would be wonderful."

"What is bothering you?" Shandra retrieved the tape and sat back down beside her aunt.

"Nothing to concern you."

"If it concerns you, it concerns me." Shandra peered into her aunt's dark brown eyes.

"I'm worried my boys will never find what their father and I have."

"They're young yet. Look at me. I'm closer to forty

than twenty which is closer to your sons' ages. They have time."

"Martin and I married when I was nineteen and he was twenty-two. We'd dated off and on in high school and out. I knew on the first date I was going to marry him. It took a little longer to convince him." Jo smiled and her eyes glistened.

"You and Ryan have that in common. He's believed we would marry from practically the first time we met. I'm the one who took the convincing." Shandra smiled. And now they were getting married, and she couldn't think of any other person she'd want to grow old with.

Jo put an arm around her waist. "And I'm glad he did. You two are wonderful together."

Jo's cell phone jingled. She glanced at it. "It's Velma." She slid a finger across the front. "Hello?" She listened. "What a thoughtful idea. We'll be right there."

Her aunt shoved the phone back in a pocket. "Velma brought us lunch. She wanted to be here when you told Nelly. Wendy came with her to take your measurements." Jo stood and led the way back to her office.

Velma stood at the door, waiting impatiently for them. "Where were you? Wendy spent ten minutes looking for you before I called." She held up a brown bag and backed up revealing Wendy. "The chicken strips are going to be cold. I hate cold chicken strips. When the heat goes so does the flavor."

Shandra glanced at Jo. Her aunt was having as much trouble keeping a straight face as she was.

"We were watching Jo and Martin's wedding video to give me an idea of what to expect." Shandra followed her two aunts into the office.

Jo continued to cross the small room to a door on the other side. She returned with two bottles of water and two sodas. She handed the sodas to Velma and Wendy and a water to Shandra.

Velma shoved everything to the side of the desk and pulled out red and white checkered paper boats heaped with chicken strips. "I sprung for a boat of jojos, too." She placed that on the desk closest to her. Then she set out little plastic containers of white and pink sauce.

The smell of the greasy strips of chicken and spicy jojos made Shandra's stomach growl. "I didn't think I was hungry until I smelled this."

"Leave it to Velma to know when to bring food," Jo said, taking one of the boats.

"What's that supposed to mean?" Velma asked, narrowing her eyes.

"That you always know when a person needs food," Jo said, before taking a bite.

"What is that blanket you have next to you?" Shandra asked Wendy.

"The doeskin is wrapped in it. I thought you might like to see what I'll make your dress out of." Wendy folded back a corner of the blanket and revealed the whitest doeskin Shandra had ever seen.

"It's beautiful." She wanted to run her hand over it to see if the material felt as soft as it looked but didn't dare get a speck of grease on the hide. "I can't wait to see what you do with this."

"As soon as you finish eating, I'll measure you. I need to get started right away to have this ready by the wedding." Wendy shoved her remaining food toward her mother. "You can have the rest. I've had enough." She stood. "I'm going to wash my hands." Her cousin left the room.

Shandra and her aunts talked about the upcoming events at the community center. When she couldn't take another bite, Shandra shoved her nearly empty boat to the middle of the desk. "I'm going to wash my hands."

Out in the hall, she didn't see her cousin. Wendy wasn't in the small restroom either. Wondering where she could have gone, Shandra took a detour by the large plate glass windows at the front of the building and glanced into the parking lot. The jacked-up pickup she'd seen earlier was there and it looked like two people were entwined in one another's arms inside the vehicle. Maybe the young man and woman who had been arguing before came to their senses.

She walked back into the office.

Wendy hadn't returned.

A glance at the clock on the wall said it was one o'clock. "Nelly should be showing up any minute." Shandra walked over to where she'd left the certificate and the packet.

A young woman walked through the door.

"Pim, what are you doing here?" Aunt Jo asked.

Shandra had to believe it was the young woman her aunt had wanted to receive the scholarship. Pim was an unusual name.

"I wanted to find out where this Friday's SYEP workshop is being held," the young woman said.

"Down in the gym," Aunt Jo said, her brow furrowed.

"Thanks." Pim faced Shandra. "You must be

Shandra Higheagle. Thank you so much for sponsoring a scholarship for young women of this reservation."

"You're welcome. What is a SYEP workshop?" Shandra asked, wondering if it really was a coincidence the young woman showed up now as they waited for Nelly to arrive.

"It's the Summer Youth Employment Program. We work for minimum wage four days a week and on Fridays we have workshops on different jobs. If I don't get help to go to college, at least I'll have some knowledge to hopefully get a better than minimum wage job." Pim waved to Jo. "Thanks!"

When the young woman was out of the office and earshot, Shandra glanced at her aunts. "Where is the workshop usually held?"

"Here," Jo said.

Shandra and Jo turned to Velma as Wendy walked into the room. "Did you tell her what was happening at one today?" they said in unison.

"I only called Nelly and told her to come here at one." Velma snorted and pointed to the clock. "She's late. You should have just handed that stuff over to Pim."

"There could be a good reason she isn't here yet," Shandra said.

"Like she's out stealing someone's boyfriend," Wendy said under her breath.

Shandra turned to her cousin. "What are you talking about?"

"Nelly tried to steal Tripp away from me. Just because she puts out, she thinks every male will fall for her." Wendy pulled out a tape measure. "I might as well get your measurements while you wait."

Shandra didn't like the fact Nelly was late and that Wendy believed it was because the other woman was sleeping with someone. Seeing Nelly's application for the scholarship, Shandra had hoped the young woman had changed her ways.

She stood with her arms out as Wendy measured and wrote down the measurements. "Would you like to feel your dress?" Wendy asked.

Shandra ran her hand over the supple doeskin. "I can't believe how soft this is. Wendy you did a wonderful job tanning the hide."

"With the leftover pieces, Aunt Jo is going to make you a pair of moccasins." Wendy covered up the leather.

A man with long braids, sweating brow, and worry etched on his face, stepped into the office. "Jo, call the police. Nelly Bingham's been stabbed."

Chapter Three

Shandra's heart raced. Why would anyone want to hurt Nelly? Her gaze landed on Wendy. The woman looked surprised but not horrified.

"Where is she?" Shandra asked the man.

"Down by the sweat lodge." The man shook his head. "It will have to be purified before we can use it now."

Shandra grabbed Velma's wrist. "Show me."

"This isn't good," Velma said, huffing.

Velma led the way out of the Community Center and down a road to the west of the building.

Shandra saw a fenced in area. "Why didn't he call for help instead of leaving her there by herself?" Frustration banged at Shandra.

"Old Moses doesn't believe in cell phones." Velma stopped at the opening in the fence and pointed.

To the right of the gate, Nelly lay face down in a pool of blood.

Shandra wanted to check her to see if she was still alive, but also didn't want to ruin anything that would help catch her killer.

Velma put a hand on Shandra's shoulder. "She's gone."

"How do you know?" She shook her aunt's hand off and took a step.

Velma grasped her arm, stopping any forward motion. "I know."

Shandra spun around to stare at the woman as sirens wailed in the distance. The shrill sound grew closer as she continued to peer into her aunt's eyes. Velma had seen Nelly's spirit leave her body.

She returned her gaze to the young woman she'd planned to have as her first scholarship recipient. Nelly's fingers were curved as if she were digging into the ground. Shandra studied her arms and feet. Nelly appeared to have been crawling toward the gate. She was a fighter right down to the end, trying to find someone to help her.

From what Shandra could see of the young woman's clothing, she had been the woman arguing with the young man this morning in the community center parking lot. If only I had realized you were the woman, I would have been looking for you. Sorrow for the woman's lost life and the impression she could have prevented this overwhelmed Shandra.

She shook off the notion as a car slid to a stop outside the fence, pluming a cloud of dust into the air.

Officer Logan Rider unfolded out of the tribal police vehicle. He stood close to seven feet, broad shoulders, barrel chest, and had a round jovial face with a smile as broad as the Cheshire cat.

"Shandra! Heard you were coming to visit. My grandmother hasn't stopped talking about it since Jo called and asked if you could come by." His gaze slid from her to Nelly. "Damn!"

Logan pulled out a notepad. "Did you see anything?"

"We were up at the center having lunch and waiting for her to arrive for a meeting," Velma said.

"She had an appointment with you?" Logan stared at Shandra.

She nodded. "Yes. We were going to make her the first recipient of my scholarship." Tears burned the backs of her eyes. "I didn't even get a chance to tell her how proud I was."

Velma put an arm around Shandra. "She worked hard after you talked to her."

"What time was her appointment?" he asked.

"One."

He glanced at his watch. "It's two-thirty now. Did you come looking for her?"

"Old Moses burst into Jo's office and said he found her. Me and Shandra came to see if we could help." Velma murmured something in Nez Perce and added, "We were too late."

"You two need to step outside the fence, please. I have photos to take and I need to place a call to the feds." Logan herded them out of the enclosure.

Shandra shuddered. "Not that man Weatherly again." The FBI agent had nearly caused Ryan's death by going back and digging up old cases after recognizing him.

"He's no longer in the agency." Logan grinned.

"I'm glad they put another agent here in his place."

The officer shook his head. "Not this agency. He's no longer in the FBI. Word is he let information leak about an undercover cop and he was tossed out."

He'd gotten what he deserved for digging up Ryan's undercover identity. "Can't say as I'm sorry for him."

"Me either. He always acted like he was better than everyone on this reservation." Logan walked over to his vehicle and began talking on the radio.

"I need to get back to Wendy. She has to go home," Velma said.

"You can't go. You have to stay here and answer questions." Shandra shielded her eyes, staring back toward the center. "Where do you think Moses is? He should be down here, too."

"I'll take my car keys to Wendy and get Moses." Velma took off back toward the center in long strides.

"Where is she going?" Logan called from over by his car.

"To give her keys to Wendy, so she can go home, and to get Moses." She had a feeling there had been something else on Velma's mind.

Shandra shifted her position to where she could see into the area and study the body position and anything that looked out of place. Had she known her attacker? Had she put up a fight? She studied the clothing. There appeared to be a rip at the shoulder of her shirt. As if someone had grabbed her sleeve to make her stop or keep her from getting away.

She studied the area. "Why here?"

"Why here what?" Logan asked, stopping beside her. He held a camera in his hands.

"Why was she attacked here? Did someone lure her?" Shandra drew her attention from the enclosure and the body. "I saw her and a young man arguing in the center parking lot earlier today."

"Why didn't you go looking for her sooner if you knew she was at the center this morning?" Logan stared at her without his usual grin.

"At the time, I didn't know it was her. All I saw was her back. She has on the same clothes."

"What did the man look like?" Logan shoved the camera in a vest pocket and pulled out his notepad.

"Tall, thin, long hair—"

"That's half the population on the reservation," Logan interrupted.

"He drove off in a dark blue jacked-up pickup that looked pretty new." She chastised herself. "No plate. I just thought it was a lover's quarrel and didn't think anything of it until I realized Nelly was the young woman he was arguing with."

"Few people write down plate numbers or even think they should." He shoved the notepad back in his pocket and pulled out the camera. "I'm going to take photos, you can leave when Velma gets back and I take her statement."

She nodded and found a place to stand in the shade where she could watch Logan work and see the area. Her heart stopped beating. What about Fawn, Nelly's daughter? Shandra thought back to the time she'd visited Nelly at her grandmother's home. It hadn't been the best place to raise a child then and with her mother gone, it would be even worse now.

Velma arrived with Old Moses on her heels.

"What will happen to Nelly's little girl, Fawn?" Shandra asked.

Velma shrugged. "If Birdie don't want to take care of her, she'll go to children's services and be fostered out."

Shandra didn't like the idea of the little girl being in foster care, but she wasn't part of the reservation and wasn't ready to take on a child at this time. And there was Ryan to consider. They were getting married and while they both knew she was getting on the older side for becoming pregnant, they had talked of children. Just not right now.

"What is the foster system like here?" she asked as Logan walked over to them.

"Velma, I'll take your statement. Then you and Shandra can go." Logan led her aunt over to his car as the ambulance pulled down the road to the fenced area.

Moses greeted the woman. "Hó. You will not be able to help her today."

"Hó, Uncle." The woman pulled the gurney toward the body.

"Wait!" Logan yelled, leaving Velma and hurrying over. "I haven't finished with the photos yet." He smiled at the woman. "Judy, you may wait in your air-conditioned vehicle. I have to finish getting Velma's statement and then your uncle's before I can finish taking the photos."

Shandra wanted to offer to take the photos but knew she wouldn't be allowed near the body anymore now that an investigation had started.

Logan wandered back over to Velma. Shandra sidled her way over to where Moses was talking with his niece.

"I came down here to get a hose to water the grass in front of the center and found her laying just like that." Moses nodded his head, making his graying braids move up and down over his 2001 Powwow t-shirt.

"Was it the first time today, you'd come down here?" Shandra asked.

He glanced her direction.

"Was the gate open from you having been down here before or was the gate closed?" she asked.

"It was open, but it was the first time I came down here today." He shrugged. "The gate isn't always closed."

"Anyone can come and go as they please?" she asked.

He nodded. "It's sacred. People know to give it respect."

Shandra glanced over her shoulder at the body. What would this do to the sacred place?

Chapter Four

Shandra and Jo gave Velma a lift to her house before continuing to the ranch. Shandra glanced over at her aunt wondering what she was thinking. Her own thoughts had been bouncing all over the place and she wasn't sure how to express what she wanted to say.

"That poor child," Jo said, out of the blue.

"She didn't deserve to die that way." Shandra felt guilty that she'd not recognized Nelly when she saw her in the parking lot. If she had, she could have called her in and she might still be alive.

"Not her, her child. Birdie Bingham didn't do a good job raising her granddaughter, what makes anyone think she could raise a great-grandchild?" Jo's lips were in a tight line and her eyes darkened with determination.

"I agree, but from what Velma said, it looks like she'll end up in foster care." Shandra didn't like the idea of the child being placed with people she didn't know with an unknown future. However, having heard Ryan lament many times over the fate of children because of their parents' actions, she knew there was little that could be done.

"That's not a good place," Jo said again and fell into silence.

They turned down the lane to the ranch. Andy was riding a horse in the corral.

"Did you call home and tell anyone about Nelly?" Shandra asked, parking her Jeep beside her uncle's pickup.

"No." Jo slid out of the Jeep and walked toward the corral.

Shandra hopped out and jogged to catch up. She wanted to see her cousin's reaction and see if he had any ideas about who would want Nelly dead.

Andy reined his horse over to the corral fence. "How did your first day of dance go?"

With everything that had happened she'd forgotten all about learning to dance and the wedding. "Not so good. It didn't happen."

"What?" He stared at his mother. "Why not?"

"Nelly Bingham was killed." Jo's face reddened, and her eyes snapped with anger. "Someone desecrated the sweat lodge by stabbing her in the sacred area."

"Nelly?" He shook his head. "Never wanted to see that happen to her. She was getting things turned around. She'd stopped selling—"

"She was selling drugs?" Shandra jumped on what Andy had been about to say.

"She has for years. Her first boyfriend is one of the biggest dealers on the rez." Andy shook his head. "Never did know what she saw in him. Coop tagged him a slime ball from their first meeting."

"Where was that?" Shandra asked, wondering if this could be the father of Nelly's baby.

"At a party at Rebecca Lake." Andy dismounted and leaned an arm on the fence rail. "Duke is fifteen or more years older than Nelly."

"Then she was a minor when they met?" If the man was the father of her child, Fawn was better off not knowing him.

Andy nodded. "She thought she was big shit hanging out with an older man, bringing him to the parties. But he was only using her to get in with the partiers and spread his drugs around. Get people hooked. Once he was selling consistently, he dropped Nelly."

Shandra wondered if he was the true love that dropped her by the wayside that Nelly had mentioned on their previous meeting. "Was she hanging around him when she would have become pregnant?"

Andy nodded. "She accused him of being the father and wanted him to pay for things, but he said, she was a whore and slept around and he wasn't paying for someone else's problem."

"That's cold." Shandra didn't like this man.

"That's why we can't have anyone making him take the child," Jo said, pivoting and hurrying to the house.

"What's that about?" Andy asked.

"I'm not sure. But your mom is worried about Fawn going into foster care." Shandra patted the horse's nose when he stuck it over the rail. "What do you know about a tall, thin, man about Coop's age who would be arguing with Nelly and drives a jacked-up dark blue pickup?"

"That sounds like Tripp Talman." Andy grabbed the horse's reins and walked along the inside of the fence.

"Are, or were, Tripp and Nelly a couple?" Shandra asked, following around the edge of the corral.

"They were together at parties. But Tripp and Wendy are a couple." Andy opened the gate and led the horse out.

"Wendy and Tripp?" Could that be why Wendy hadn't been upset hearing about Nelly? Wendy had been absent for a while at the time someone could have stabbed Nelly. Shandra would have to do more digging into the relationships. She didn't want to believe her cousin could have killed anyone. However, when it came to jealousy, she'd discovered a lot of murders were caused by that emotion.

"Was Nelly seeing anybody beside Tripp and possibly the drug dealer?" Shandra followed Andy and the horse over to the barn.

"You know Nelly. She liked to have a good time and it didn't really matter who with." Andy's cheeks darkened as if the subject embarrassed him.

Shandra studied her cousin. "Were you one of the men?"

Andy glanced around as if he feared someone was near enough to hear what he was about to say. "I hung out with her a time or two at parties."

Shandra studied Andy. "You knew her reputation."

"When you're at a party, things like that don't matter. You're lonely and hook up with whoever is willing." He ducked his head. "I can't say I'm proud of it. But that's just the way it is."

"I'm not judging. Just asking. We need to know who would want to kill Nelly. And why." Shandra nodded to the horse. "You're doing a great job with this horse. I'll talk to you later."

Shandra wandered to the house wondering about the young woman she had picked to be her first scholarship winner. Nelly had appeared to have been someone thinking about a future to have acquired her GED and applied for the scholarship. She was a young woman who had brought a child into the world alone and was fighting for a better life for the two of them. It had to have been someone she knew that killed her.

She needed to discover what Nelly and Tripp had been arguing about. And she needed to get more information on both Tripp and the drug dealer.

Shandra entered the old farmhouse and found Jo busy baking. She'd learned from her last trip to the reservation that Jo baked when she was upset.

"I didn't realize you knew Nelly so well," Shandra said, walking over to the counter where Jo stirred something in a bowl.

Jo glanced her direction then back down to the bowl. "I didn't know Nelly that well. However, she did bring Fawn to the center quite a bit for children's activities. She might have been young and had a poor upbringing, but she was mother enough to know her daughter needed to be around other children. Her applying for a scholarship to get out of here… I just feel like her life was wasted, and I don't want the same to happen to her daughter."

Shandra put a hand on Jo's shoulder. "Do we know what will happen for sure?"

Jo shook her head. "I'm not sure what. But Birdie

is in no shape to take care of a small child."

"If the father really is the drug dealer, he has no business having her either," Shandra added.

~*~

Shandra's phone jingled a jazz tune as she was getting ready for bed. Without glancing at the phone, she knew it would be Ryan.

She picked up the phone and slid her finger across the screen. "Good evening."

"Evening, beautiful." Ryan's usual greeting always warmed her heart. "How did this first day of learning to dance and wedding planning go?"

"Not so well. We had a little hiccup that changed the events of the day."

"What do you mean?" Ryan's voice went on alert as if he were on duty. He was the skeptical policemen, always looking for the worst. Which of course this time it was.

"I told you we picked Nelly Bingham to be the recipient of my scholarship."

"Yes."

"She didn't show up for our meeting today, and the groundskeeper found her."

"What do you mean, found her?" The timbre of Ryan's voice told her he already had a good idea how they'd found poor Nelly.

"Someone killed her by the sweat lodge behind the community center. It kind of stopped anything else that was happening today."

"Shandra how do you always find the bodies?" Ryan had already drifted into his detective mode.

It was one of the things that Shandra loved about the man. No matter what was happening, he could shift into a protector of not only her, but anyone who needed protection.

"I saw her arguing with a young man earlier in the morning. Only, I didn't know it was her." She sighed. "I have a feeling my cousin Wendy might be connected to this somehow. She and Nelly were dating the same young man who turns out to be the one that Nelly was having an argument with this morning." She hoped Ryan could help her make sense of everything.

"You need to be careful. If Nelly was coming to see you, there may be a connection." His tone was assertive.

"I think it was Tripp, the young man she argued with, or it could be because she had been selling drugs." She tapped her finger against her chin. This seemed the best direction to consider.

"What do you mean she had been? It's hard to get out of that racket."

"She must have. Everyone says she was turning her life around, because I'd offered the scholarship." It made her proud that her small effort to help a woman on the reservation had made that much of an impact on Nelly. "To have applied for the scholarship she had to go through a drug test. So she wasn't using."

"Not all sellers are users. In fact, the smart ones don't use the stuff at all. They just prey on the weaker users."

"I believe she had cleaned up all of her life. She deserved the scholarship, and I feel obligated to make sure her killer is found." Shandra had felt a connection with the woman the first time they'd met and now, knowing how close Nelly had come to getting out of here and bettering her life, Shandra couldn't let go of the notion she needed to help.

"I know this is falling on deaf ears, but you should stay out of this. Let the police handle it." Ryan was smart, he didn't order her, he made a strong appeal to her need to make him happy.

"I can't promise you I can stay out of it." She acknowledged his concern but having her first recipient of the scholarship die only hours before it was even announced had shaken Shandra. There was no way she was going to be able to stay away from this investigation. And it looked like she was going to be at the reservation for more than a week.

"Shandra, leave this to the authorities. There is no sense in you getting tangled up in this so close to our wedding."

"If grandmother comes to me in a dream and gives me clues, there is no way I can stay out of this." She didn't want to go against Ryan's wishes. However, if her dreams revealed clues to help solve the crime, she would follow them, wherever they led her. Ryan had taught her to believe in them.

"We're about to start a life together. I don't want something to happen before we can say our vows." Ryan's voice had lost his persuasiveness and turned to caring.

Shandra would've laughed at how Ryan had shifted gears knowing she would dig in if he ordered her. Even knowing he cared and worried about her, she had to find the truth for Nelly. And Fawn. The little girl would one day grow up and wonder what had happened to her mother. All she would hear would be the rumors and stories of her mother bedding men and going to parties. She wanted the child to learn her mother had been on the brink of changing both their lives by going off to college and beginning a career.

"I can't make any promises."

Ryan sighed on the other end of the phone. "I'll put in for a week of leave. I'll be there this Saturday."

"You don't have to." Her knight in shining armor was coming to help her solve the murder.

"Yes, I do. Someone has to keep you out of trouble." His tone was light, but she heard conviction as well.

She smiled. Deep down, she'd known he wouldn't leave her alone to investigate this. "I look forward to you joining me."

"See you on Saturday and talk to you tomorrow."

Shandra turned the phone off, stared at the instrument in her hands, and picked up a notebook to write down everything she knew.

Chapter Five

The next morning Shandra entered the kitchen with her notepad of questions that she'd written down the night before. Jo was busy making breakfast, Uncle Martin sat at the table, sipping coffee and reading the paper. Andy was already digging into the pancakes.

Shandra took a seat alongside Andy and shoved the notebook, opened to the page with her questions, toward him.

Her cousin glanced at the page. The words caught his attention and he started reading.

"Good morning, Shandra. We'll go back to the community center this morning and get started on your dance lesson," Aunt Jo said, placing a cup of tea in front of Shandra.

"Good, I'm excited to get started. I talked with Ryan last night. He's going to come join me this Saturday. And possibly stay for a week. Will that be an inconvenience?" Shandra's gaze flicked from her aunt, to her uncle, and back to her aunt.

"You know we always enjoy having Ryan here. Is he coming because of what happened?" Aunt Jo sat down in the chair beside Shandra.

"He is. He doesn't want me to get into trouble." She laughed but the rest of her family didn't.

"He's a smart man," Uncle Martin said. He put down the paper and picked up his coffee cup taking a sip.

Andy tapped the notebook she'd laid beside him. "That's a lot of questions and what ifs." He studied her. "I'd say the first person you want to talk to is Tripp."

"Where will I find him this morning?" Shandra raised her cup of tea and sipped.

"He's one of the drummers," Aunt Jo said.

"Drummers?" Shandra glanced at her aunt.

"Yeah, he's one of the drummers for the ceremonies." Jo smiled. "He'll be one of the drummers at your wedding."

"How many drummers will there be?" Shandra asked, thinking maybe it was better to focus on her wedding and the ceremony afterwards, than asking questions about Tripp.

Andy stared at her. "Seven Drum Religion?"

"Sorry? That makes sense," Shandra said, feeling silly that she hadn't connected the number. Her mind had been on something other than the religion and ceremonies. It had been on who she should talk with and how to bring up Nelly and not get stonewalled.

"Will he be drumming while I practice?" Shandra asked.

"No, we'll be using CDs for music while you learn to step." Aunt Jo pushed the plate of pancakes toward

Shandra.

"I didn't realize ceremonial songs have been recorded." Shandra placed a pancake on her plate.

"We won't be using the ceremonial song. We'll just be using recorded music to allow you to understand the flow and the beat of the songs."

Shandra wondered how she would interpret the song when she wouldn't fully understand their meanings and what steps she would learn. She'd watched dancing at powwows and other events and had felt the beat of the drum deep within her. Had that been her heart searching and learning to beat to the sound of her people?

~*~

After breakfast had been cleaned up, Shandra was surprised Jo suggested they take her vehicle to town. It wasn't until they were driving through Nespelem that she discovered the reason why. Aunt Jo took a detour through the town and ended up in front of Nelly Bingham's house.

"Why are we here?" Shandra asked, worrying her aunt was taking Nelly's murder much too hard.

"I just want to have a little talk with Birdie." Jo open her door and slid out of the car.

Shandra wasn't about to let her aunt go in the house by herself. She had noticed Jo acting unsettled last night and this morning. Her aunt and uncle had been in a lengthy discussion late into the night. Their voices had been muffled through the bedroom floor, but she'd woke two times and heard them talking.

Aunt Jo marched up to the house and knocked on the door.

The only sound on the other side was that of a child

crying.

Jo pounded harder on the door. When no one answered, she grasped the knob. It turned. She opened the door and stepped inside. "Anybody home?" she called out.

Shandra couldn't believe the mess the house was in. She'd visited several homes on her trips to the reservation. Usually the only houses that looked this bad had drunkards living in them. In the middle of all of the mess sat the little girl. Tears streamed down her gaunt cheeks and a woeful expression tipped down her small lips.

Aunt Jo swooped down and picked the child up in her arms. "There, there darling. We'll take care of you." With the child in her arms, she wandered into the kitchen.

Shandra followed, wondering what the child was thinking as Fawn stared at her with big round eyes.

Jo opened the refrigerator, emitting nasty smells. She said something under her breath and handed the child to Shandra.

With the child clinging to her, Shandra watched her aunt open and close every door and drawer in the kitchen. Jo finally found a box of Saltines in a tin. She opened the tin, pulled out a still sealed package of crackers and opened them. She sniffed and tasted a cracker before handing the package to Shandra.

"I'm going to have a talk with Birdie." Jo marched out of the kitchen, leaving her with the child.

Fawn no longer cried. Her wide eyes studied Shandra as her tiny belly made grumbling sounds.

"When did you last eat?" Shandra held out two crackers to the child. She grabbed one in each hand and bit into one and then the other.

"I bet you're confused about what's going on." She brushed the hair out of the little girl's face as Fawn nibbled on the crackers. When she'd eaten the two crackers, Shandra handed the child another one.

Voices rose in the back of the house. The loudest voice was Birdie's, Nelly's grandmother and this child's great-grandmother. Within minutes Jo stormed back into the kitchen, plucked the little girl from her arms, and nodded for Shandra to follow her.

"What are you doing?" Shandra stayed one step behind her aunt all the way to the car. "You can't put her in the car without a children's car seat."

"It's only for a short distance. We have extras at the center. Get in. I'm putting her in your lap until we get to the center." Aunt Jo stood beside the passenger door waiting for Shandra to get in.

"You can't just take her." Shandra wasn't sure she wanted to be included in a kidnapping.

"Birdie agreed I can take better care of Fawn than she can." Aunt Jo gave her a stern look. "Get in."

Not knowing reservation protocol, Shandra asked, "Is that legal?"

"It is if the family agrees. In this case the only family is Birdie. I'll call children's services and your cousin Liz when we get to the center. Liz can draw up legal papers. As long as there is someone willing to take in the child, the family doesn't care, and children's services doesn't have to step in, everyone is happy." Aunt Jo nodded to the open car door. "Get in."

Unsure if her uncle knew about Jo's interest in the child, Shandra opened the door, slid in, buckled herself, and opened her arms to take Fawn.

Aunt Jo placed the child on Shandra's lap, closed the door, and went around to the driver side and slid in. "That is no place for this, or any, child to grow up."

~*~

At the center, Jo placed Fawn in the daycare and marched off to make her phone calls. Shandra wandered around the community center, waiting for her aunt to take care of Fawn's future and be ready to help with her upcoming wedding.

The sounds of sneakers squeaking on the gymnasium floor caught Shandra's attention. She walked down the ramp into the gymnasium and was pleased to discover Tripp and several other young men playing basketball. Unsure how to start up a conversation with her cousin's boyfriend, Shandra found a chair along the wall by the door and sat down to watch.

One by one, the young men noticed her. They all started taking risky shots and fouling recklessly. She chuckled at how they were showing off because she watched. Finally, Tripp moved away from the others, heading toward bottles of water by a pile of street clothes.

Shandra took this opportunity to start up a conversation. The bottles and clothing were only a short distance from where she sat.

"Are you practicing for something important?" Shandra asked, catching his attention.

Tripp stopped drinking water, turned his head her direction, and smiled. He walked toward her. "No, we're just practicing." He stopped only a few feet from her. "Are you new? I'm sure I would've remembered you."

Shandra was surprised that this young man wasn't as cautious as her cousins and their friends had been the first time she'd visited the community center. "I'm here visiting."

He smiled as his friends came over to join them.

"Who are you visiting?" Tripp placed his body between her and his friends.

"Jo Elwood. She's my aunt." She stifled a giggle when Tripp's eyebrows raised almost to his hairline. "I'm here preparing for my wedding."

"I know. Wendy is making your dress. It's going to be a traditional wedding." Tripp relaxed, allowing his friends to gather closer.

"Jo told me you will be one of the drummers."

"Is that what you want to talk to me about? About the songs that will be played?"

Shandra could tell Tripp believed in his music and the ceremonies of their people. "That and…" she glanced at the three other men, "I wondered why you and Nelly were arguing in this parking lot yesterday morning?"

Tripp started to back away from her, but Shandra followed not allowing him the chance to run away. "I saw you two arguing. If you don't tell me what it was about I'm going to tell the police."

"Ooooo," his friends said, mocking her threat.

She glared at them and turned her anger on Tripp. "Which do you fear more? The police or Wendy knowing about you and Nelly?"

Tripp put his hands up and shook his head. "Our argument had nothing to do with what happened to her."

"How do you know that? It could have had

everything to do with what happened to her." Shandra wasn't going to let anyone, including her cousin, get away with murder.

Tripp turned to his friends. "Give us some space." They all nodded and went back to playing ball. The sound of sneakers squeaking and the ball bouncing went on for several seconds before Tripp shifted his attention back to her.

"Nelly and I had some good times. But I don't love her. I was trying to tell her that. She had some notion that I should go with her to Spokane when she went to school." He put his hands in his pockets, walked three steps away, and walked back. His face was wrinkled in consternation.

"Why would she have the idea that you loved her or the two of you were a couple?" Shandra didn't like the idea that her cousin, Wendy, was being played by this young man.

"I don't know." His face was the perfect portrait of disbelief and confusion. "When we hooked up, she acted like it was no big thing. Then when I told her I didn't want to hook up anymore, that I was getting serious with Wendy, she got all angry at me. She shouted she was going to tell Wendy all the things we did. That I wasn't good enough for her and tell her lies about things that we didn't do." He pulled his hands out of his pocket and held them out, imploring. "Wendy knows that I hooked-up with Nelly a time or two at parties. Wendy doesn't party. She's traditional all the way. That's what I love about her. Her tradition. But Nelly didn't understand."

Shandra studied the young man. His facial features had softened, tender even, as he spoke of Wendy and his love for her. She hoped for her cousin's sake that he did love her and he had stopped his roaming way.

"Nelly was here trying to get you to move to Spokane with her?" Shandra asked.

Tripp nodded his head.

"Why yesterday? Was that the first time she'd mentioned you moving to Spokane?"

"She knew she had gotten your scholarship. That's all she talked about the last time we were together. Getting her GED and getting the hell out of here." He shook his head. "She never mentioned wanting me to go with her." He peered into her eyes. "If she had I would have told her no then."

"What about her daughter? Was she going to take Fawn with her?" How had the young woman planned to go to school and live and take care of her daughter at the same time?

"I don't know. I figured she'd leave her with her grandmother or the father." The look of disgust and disdain the man had for the two people he'd just mentioned was clearly written on his face. From the pinched lips to the shudder.

"Do you know who Fawn's father is?" Shandra asked.

He laughed. "Everyone knows. It's that parasite Duke Waters. She told everyone when she was pregnant as if that would make him take them in. He doesn't care for anyone but himself and the dollar."

"Where could I find Duke?" she asked.

Tripp's head snapped around and he studied her. "You don't want to find him."

It looked like she'd go visit Duke after Ryan arrived. "Okay, then did Nelly have any girlfriends who would have moved to Spokane with her?"

"Why do you think she was after me? She didn't have anyone. She slept around making the girls all hate her." Tripp nodded toward his friends. "I'm getting back to my game."

She let him go. But he wasn't crossed off her list. He admitted to having an argument with Nelly and she had threatened to tell his girlfriend lies. Nelly, Nelly, I thought you had changed. Or were you so desperate to have someone go with you, that you resorted to the only thing you could think of?

Chapter Six

At noon Aunt Jo brought Fawn up to her office and the three of them had sandwiches. The happiness shining in Jo's eyes, told Shandra the meeting with the social worker and Liz had gone well.

"Does Uncle Martin know what you did?" Shandra asked, pointing at Fawn with a potato chip.

"He does," Uncle Martin said from the office door. He walked over to Jo and peered down at the child. "Your aunt has wanted a daughter for a long time. After Andy's rough birth, the doctor suggested we not have any more." He glanced at his wife. Love shone like beacons from his eyes. "She now has her wish."

Jo squeezed his hand. "Thank you for indulging me this wish."

"I can't say no to you." He knelt on the floor next to Fawn who had been playing with a paper clip dispenser. "How would you like to come with me? I have a pony who has been asking to see you."

The child's eyes lit up for the first time since this

morning. "A pony?" she whispered.

"Yes. Her name is Princess and she's been wanting to meet you." Martin winked at Jo over the child's head.

"Princess? Really?" Fawn spun and slapped her hands and forearms in Aunt Jo's lap. "Can I see Princess Pony?"

Jo ran a hand down the child's face. "Of course, you can. You can see Princess Pony every day, you'll be coming to live with Uncle Martin, Andy, and I. Would you like that?"

The child's eyes teared up. "Mommy isn't coming back."

"That's right. Your mommy had a bad accident. She can't come back. But we'd love to have you come live with us. We have horses, lots of land, and a room just for you." Aunt Jo's eyes glistened with tears. Only the white knuckles as she gripped the arms of the chair showed how much the child's answer meant to her.

"I see pony and live with you." She flung her small arms around Jo and hugged.

"Come on then, Princess is waiting." Uncle Martin held out his hand. Fawn clutched two fingers and waved at us as they walked out of the room.

"That's a good man you have there, Aunt Jo." Shandra could barely say the words for the lump in her throat.

"I knew that the minute I laid eyes on him all those years ago." She sniffed. "I have the conference room reserved for your first lesson. When your food has settled let me know."

Shandra studied her aunt. The woman had more grace, love, and strength than anyone she'd ever met.

"Don't you think we need to get some clothes and things for Fawn? And which room is hers?"

Jo smiled. "I called your cousin Sylvia. She's taking her daughter's outgrown clothes to the ranch today. Velma rounded up some toys and Andy moved into the barn. He's been threatening to do it for a while now. Claims he's too old to be living at home." She laughed. "I guess in the barn he feels he has privacy."

"When did you talk to all of these people?" Shandra couldn't believe what her aunt had accomplished in a short amount of time.

"Last night. I asked Martin what he thought, he agreed, and I called everyone. I just had to persuade Birdie it was the right thing to do." Jo scowled.

"Was Birdie really okay with you taking her great-granddaughter?"

"It seems someone has been slipping money into her mailbox once a month since the birth of Fawn. She was more worried about losing the money than the child."

Shandra sat up straight. "Do you think it was Duke making what he considered a restitution for having fathered a child?"

"That or someone else felt guilty." Aunt Jo's eyes held a determined glint to them. "I will make sure that child is loved and never knows her mother was anything other than a loving mother."

Shandra stood. "Come on. I'm ready to learn about dancing." When her aunt stood, Shandra put an arm around her shoulders and squeezed. "You are the best thing to happen to that little girl."

She just hoped Duke didn't try to take the child away.

Dangerous Dance

~*~

"Listen to the beat. It is the heart of our people.
You dance to the beat and feel it in your bones." Aunt
Jo raised the volume on the drum song playing. She
grasped Shandra's hand and led her to the middle of the
room. When they'd first entered the room, they'd
shoved the tables against the walls and placed the chairs
on top.

"Hear the heartbeat." Jo closed her eyes, listened,
and her feet began moving, pressing into the ground
with each beat that reverberated off the walls of the
small room.

Shandra tried to listen to the beat, follow it with her
heart and her feet, but her mind kept circling to Nelly.
She'd expected grandmother to come to her in a dream
last night. But she hadn't and now she would need to
bring her into a dream.

"What are they saying?" she asked. Her feet slowly
picking up the beat but wondering at the singing.

"They aren't saying words. It is only sounds." Aunt
Jo stopped and studied her. "You aren't putting all of
your heart into this."

"I can't concentrate on my wedding knowing there
is someone, perhaps someone we know, who coldly
killed Nelly." A shiver raced up her spine at the thought
it could be someone they knew.

"Then dance and ask for help in solving the murder
so you can enjoy your wedding."

Shandra stopped hopping from foot to foot and
watched her aunt. She meant what she said. Could
dancing help her find guidance? Shrugging, Shandra
listened to the music, focusing on the beats, she pressed
her feet to the floor with the same calm and preciseness

as Jo.

Her mind centered on the beat, the voices became a white noise in the background. White, fluffy clouds drifted into her thoughts. One by one they captured her questions and floated out of her head toward the sky.

The drums grew louder, the voices more insistent. The beat resounded in her body, from her feet touching the ground, up her legs, through her body, and into her heart and mind. Visions of her ancestors dancing around a fire. Grandmother stood behind the dancers, her arms open as if embracing the ceremony.

I must talk to you. Shandra beseeched her grandmother.

Her grandmother shook her head, the music faded, and her steps failed. Shandra stumbled backwards.

Aunt Jo caught her in her arms. "Did you trip?"

"Why wouldn't she talk to me?"

"Who?" Aunt Jo turned the music off.

"Grandmother."

Her aunt studied her. "You saw mother while you were dancing?"

Shandra shook out of the memory and glanced at her aunt. The look on Jo's face told her to not say too much. While Aunt Jo understood Shandra had certain abilities, it was clear she didn't fully comprehend them.

"I saw many people dancing around a fire."

Jo picked up the cd case and pointed to the first song. *Fire Song.*

Another chill chased down her spine. She needed to talk to Velma. "I think this is enough dancing for today. I'll call Velma and have her pick me up."

Aunt Jo shook her head. "I'll drop you off there. I can leave for the day."

They put the conference room back together and headed to the office to pick up their purses and for Jo to log out.

Pim Solomon, the runner up for Shandra's scholarship, stood at the entry of the building, reading the bulletin board.

Shandra followed Jo into the office, wondering if the young woman always spent this much time at the center. Jo turned off her computer and pulled open the desk drawer where she kept her purse. Shandra opened the door to the storage room to get her fringed bag.

Turning from closing the door, she found Pim standing in the office doorway.

"Good afternoon, Pim. Do you need something from me?" Jo asked.

The young woman's face deepened in color. "I-I hate to ask, but mom was wondering if you were going to pick a second choice for the scholarship since, you know, Nelly can't use it."

Shandra stared at the young woman. Did she know she was the runner-up, or just hoping she had finished close to the top and might have a chance at the scholarship?

"To not dishonor Nelly's passing, I'll make the formal announcement next week about who will receive the scholarship." She hadn't thought of anything beyond Nelly's killer should be found. Holding off until next week seemed like the most plausible thing to do, given the circumstances.

"Okay, sounds good." She continued to stand in the door.

"We're on our way out," Jo said, walking toward the only exit from the room.

"Oh, of course." Pim backed up. "Do you need help with anything?"

"We're good," Shandra said.

"Okay. I'll finish reading the activities. Thank you for your answer." Pim walked stiffly over to the bulletin board and acted as if she were enthralled by the events posted there.

Outside, Shandra asked her aunt, "Is she always that…awkward?"

"As she grows older her shyness and social skills make her appear awkward. She has a brilliant mind. Top of her class when she graduated." Jo unlocked her car.

Shandra's gaze traveled to the fenced in sweat lodge down below the community center. She really wanted to have a better look around today. It didn't appear as if the police had put up crime scene tape.

"I think I'll have a look around and call Velma."

Jo stopped lowering into her car and stood. "I don't like you nosing around alone. What would Ryan say?"

"Have back up." Shandra pulled out her phone and dialed Velma.

"Shandra, I was just thinking about you," Velma said.

She'd discovered when Velma had a sight or dream her voice had a different timbre to it. That's what she heard now. "Then you know I would like you to come to the community center and help me look around down by the sweat lodge."

"That's not what I was thinking, and you shouldn't be either. Looking into murders in a sacred place is not good for anyone." Velma's words might have sounded against the adventure, but her tone held excitement.

"I'll be down by the sweat lodge when you get here." Shandra terminated the conversation and smiled at Jo. "She'll be here soon. Go home and check on Fawn."

"I don't like leaving you here alone." Jo started to lower herself into her car.

"I'll only be alone for ten-fifteen minutes the way Velma drives." Shandra closed the door on her aunt. "I'll see you whenever Velma can drop me off."

She watched her aunt drive out of the parking lot and turn onto the highway before facing the road down to the sweat lodge. She wasn't sure what she'd find but there had to be a clue there somewhere. It was obvious from her experience while dancing, grandmother wasn't going to help.

Chapter Seven

The gate to the fence around the sweat lodge was locked. Could that be why the police didn't have up crime tape? Shandra walked to the right of the gate, following the outside of the privacy fence. She noted the small pieces of trash that must have blown up against the base of the fencing since it was installed. They were all dirty or wrinkled from having been rained on. There didn't seem to be anything new. She'd hoped whoever killed Nelly had waited and in doing so, left behind evidence.

She'd walked the perimeter when a plume of dust appeared on the road from the community center to the sweat lodge. Glancing up, she spotted Velma's car. The woman was going to be disappointed when they couldn't even get through the gate.

The car stopped. Velma eased her husky six feet out of the older model luxury car. "I expected to find you inside," she said, marching up to Shandra.

"The gate's locked." Shandra pointed to the

padlock and chain.

Velma dug into her purse and pulled out two paper clips that had been bent in different ways. "I've had to get into and out of places where no one wanted me a few times in my life." She walked up to the padlocked gate and shoved the ends of the clips into the lock. With the finesse Shandra used when forming her clay vases, Velma jiggled and cajoled the lock.

A smile spread across her face as the lock sprung open. The smile was as quick to disappear when Shandra reached out to open the gate. "You do know until this area is cleansed anyone who enters could be asking for bad fortune to follow them?"

"This is the only way I know to help discover who killed Nelly. I need to see the inside and see if the police missed anything when looking for evidence." Shandra slipped through the gate. Her gaze landed on the bloody spot where Nelly had lain.

"Moses said the gate was open when he found her. But did he mean open or unlocked?" She glanced over her shoulder at Velma. She stood just inside the gate, not moving.

"He didn't say which. Why?"

"If the gate were closed and unlocked why would Nelly come in here unless someone had asked her to meet them here. Moses said it isn't always locked. I would think that would leave the community center open to get sued if anyone were hurt on the premises."

"No one here would think of that. If it were a Federal building or someone other than an Indian who owned the place, then they would think, I can get money. But not our own. We know pockets are empty." Velma shrugged. "Even though we are supposed to schedule the use of the sweat lodge through the community center, there are many elders who use it when they feel like it." She sniffed. "And I've heard some of the young people have used it to meet up, if you know what I mean."

Shandra had a good idea she knew what Velma meant. Had Nelly set up an assignation here before coming to accept her scholarship? But with who? Tripp had turned her down, or so he said. Could he have had one last fling with her and then silenced her? And what about the way she was killed?

She hoped Ryan would be able to access the information the police gathered.

The sound of dirty brakes screeching caught her attention. "Is someone coming?"

Velma spun around and peered out through the privacy slats. "Looks like a fed and Logan." She finally left the gate, hurrying across the space between them. "We have to hide. They'll take one look at that lock and know we picked it to get in here."

"Your car is parked out there. Logan knows it by sight. It will make us look guilty if we hide." Shandra put up a braver front than she felt. Ryan had told her to stay out of things and now she was going to be caught by an FBI agent and a tribal officer she respected. But she had the feeling he wouldn't respect her as much when he found her at his crime scene.

The gate rattled and opened.

A tall, broad shouldered man with a brown, bald head, narrowed eyes, and disapproving grimace on his face, walked through the gate followed by Logan.

"Shandra and Velma, what are you doing in here? This is a crime scene, off limits and locked." Logan held up the lock. "Was locked. Which one of you is the lock picker?"

Shandra didn't want her aunt to get in trouble. She lived on the reservation, Shandra was just visiting. "I did. I wanted to—"

The FBI agent held up his hand to stop her. "You do know this is a federal case? You could be thrown in jail for tampering with evidence."

She took a step toward the man. "I-we didn't tamper with anything. We're just looking."

He motioned with his hand. "You're walking around, leaving footprints."

"So did Logan," she motioned to the police officer, "…the EMTs, the medical examiner, and any other officers who were here collecting evidence."

Logan shook his head as if to say she needed to stop speaking.

"This is federal jurisdiction. Who are you?" The man pulled out what she presumed was his cell phone.

"Shandra Higheagle."

"She's just visiting, it's my fault," Velma chimed in.

"And you are?" the FBI agent asked.

"Velma Wilbur, Shandra's aunt and member of one of the oldest families on this reservation." She puffed out her chest and stood taller, making her an inch taller than the man questioning her.

The agent narrowed his eyes. "You can't sway me with who you are related to. You have both violated a sealed off area." He whipped his gaze to Shandra. "You two were found with the body by Officer Ryder. Did you come back for the murder weapon?"

While she was glad to see the man was diligent

with his desire to work the murder, she didn't like him immediately thinking she and Velma were suspects. "We didn't come for the weapon. I wanted to get a better look around and try to figure out what happened. Nelly had an appointment to meet with Velma and I in the community center. We were worried about her when she didn't show, then the groundskeeper came to the office and said he'd found her. We came down to see if we could help."

"That was yesterday, why are you here today?" the agent asked.

"To make sense of it all." She wasn't going to give him any more information than that.

Logan's eyebrows rose.

"You need to leave." The agent held the gate open.

Velma glanced at her. Shandra nodded, and they marched out of the enclosure. She didn't like that they had been banned from the one place that might give them clues.

"Where can we find Duke Waters?" Shandra asked Velma when they were both settled in the car.

Her aunt's head spun so fast, Shandra heard her neck pop. "Duke Waters? Why would you want to see that no good scum ball?"

"To ask him what he plans to do about Fawn. I don't want Aunt Jo getting attached and have the man decide he does want to play daddy." She knew playing on her aunt's emotions would get more help out of Velma than telling her she wanted to ask him about Nelly's involvement with his drug dealing. She'd planned to wait to contact him until Ryan arrived, but he was the only other reasonable person who would have wanted Nelly dead, besides Tripp.

"I'm not sure where he hangs out during the day, but we both know someone who might know." She backed the car up and headed out to the highway.

"Who?"

"Billy Crow."

"I thought he was an alcoholic who didn't do drugs." She remembered the young man she'd wheedled information out of when Coop was charged with a murder.

"He also knows everything that happens on the reservation because everyone believes he is a drunk and won't remember what he sees and hears." Velma eased off the highway and into Nespelem. Within minutes she parked in the Ketch Pen parking lot. For early afternoon there were quite a few vehicles.

Velma groaned.

"What? Isn't he here?" Shandra studied the vehicles trying to remember what his pickup had looked like.

"Billy's here. So is Jessie."

Shandra did an internal groan as well. Jessie Lawyer had been infatuated with Shandra's father, tried to seduce her uncle, and was the biggest lush she'd ever met. "Well, we can hope she is on the opposite side of the room as Billy."

They slipped out of the car, walked to the building, and pushed the door open.

Shandra stood just inside the door a few seconds, allowing her eyes to adjust to the dim interior after the bright sunlight. The place hadn't changed. Same posters and photographs on the walls. Her gaze went straight to the photo of her dad riding a bucking horse. The lights hanging over the pool tables and the one over the bar gave out the most lighting in the place.

"We should go home and go back to bed," Velma said at her shoulder.

"Why?"

"This isn't our day. We get caught by the police and now this." She pointed.

Shandra followed the length of Velma's arm and beyond her finger to Jessie and Billy sitting at a table together.

This time she groaned outwardly and walked to the table.

Billy glanced up. He smiled but it wasn't one of recognition, just a happy, drunken welcome.

Jessie narrowed her eyes. "I know you."

Shandra took the seat next to Billy, leaving Velma to sit beside Jessie. "I was hoping you could help me with something," she said to Billy.

"Me? What would I know?" He downed the last of the beer in his mug.

She motioned for the waitress to bring him another. "I'm trying to find Duke Waters."

"What the hell you looking for him for?" Jessie shrieked. "He's my man, you keep your hands off him."

Shandra leaned back from the woman's spittle and red angry eyes. "I only want to ask him some questions. Are you and Duke friends?"

"He's been in my bed."

"Who hasn't?" Velma said under her breath.

"What? What did you say you old battle axe?" Jessie turned her angry eyes on Velma.

"Battle Axe, you're older than me and much too worn to say you slept with a younger man," Velma leaned toward the drunk woman, making her lean back and sputter.

Shandra put her hand on Velma's arm, hoping she understood to relax. "I just want to know how to contact Duke to ask him two questions." She turned her attention on Billy.

"He's been hanging out at the Twelve Tribes Casino in Omak. Found a new…" he shot a glance at Jessie, "he's been working out of there lately."

"Duke's the best thing that ever happened to me," Jessie said.

"What about your husband? Shouldn't he be the best thing?" Velma asked.

Jessie stared at her wide-eyed. "Husband?"

"Frank Lawyer, the man you married twenty years ago." Velma glared at the woman.

"He's no husband. He won't take me to bed." Jessie raised her glass of beer as if in a toast.

Shandra waited for the waitress to bring over the beer. She paid for it and stood. "Thank you, Billy. Good seeing you again, Jessie."

The woman stared at her as if trying to remember.

Velma rose out of her chair and headed for the door. Outside, she asked, "We're not going to the casino, are we?"

"No. I'll go with Ryan on Saturday. Do you believe Jessie that she slept with Duke?"

"If that man thought he could get her hooked on his product, I wouldn't doubt it." Velma slid in behind the wheel of her car. "I'm taking you to Jo's. I'm tired of all these surprises."

Shandra laughed and buckled her seat belt. "You didn't see all of this coming?"

"No." Velma glanced her way as she backed out of

the parking lot. "What has your grandmother said about this?"

"Nothing. She came to me when I was dancing this morning, but she basically refused to show me anything." Shandra turned slightly in the seat and studied her aunt. "Do you think she's mad at me for trying to solve Nelly's murder?"

"No. She would want justice. Maybe she was trying to tell you something else." Velma pulled the car out onto the highway.

Shandra closed her eyes and tried to remember what she'd seen. Nothing came to her.

Chapter Eight

Dinner that night was fun. Shandra watched as her aunt, uncle and cousin all tried to make the child, Fawn, feel at home and important.

The little girl ate everything Jo put on her plate and smiled at Martin and Andy as if they were her best friends.

"Did you meet Princess?" Shandra asked.

Fawn's whole face lit up and she smiled. "She have white spots."

"Fawn is going to be a great cowgirl, she sat on Princess and wasn't afraid," Uncle Martin said, smiling.

The little girl nodded her head.

"That sounds like fun. Maybe we can go riding together while I'm here," Shandra said.

Fawn shook her head. "Momma say don't go strangers."

Shandra was once again struck by what a good mother Nelly had been. "I'm not a stranger. Jo is my aunt, Martin is my uncle, and this guy here is my cousin," she said, pointing a thumb toward Andy. "We're family now."

Fawn scrunched her face as if thinking. "Like Mawmaw Birdie and Uncle Tripp and Uncle Duke?"

Shandra glanced at her aunt. Duke had been in the child's life and so had Tripp, Wendy's boyfriend. "Yes, like Mawmaw and your uncles."

The child's face brightened. "We can ride." She clapped her little hands together.

"You have to practice first in the corral," Andy said, already behaving like a protective big brother.

"In corral," Fawn said, smiling and picking up a green bean.

A jazz tune sounded in the distance.

Her phone.

Shandra excused herself from the table and hurried over to where she'd placed her purse on the couch in the living room.

Ryan.

"Hello," she answered.

"Hi, beautiful." He cleared his throat. "I just had a conversation with my friend in the FBI."

The insinuation in his voice had her cringing. He knew she and Velma broke into the crime scene. "Did you find out anything?"

He laughed. "You know I found out you and Velma picked a lock to get into an FBI crime scene. What were you two thinking?"

"I just wanted a look around. But the FBI and Logan arrived too soon." She wasn't going to apologize for trying to help solve Nelly's murder.

"That's Special Agent Troy Tremaine. Word has it he is a stickler for everything going by the book. You might want to keep away from him." Ryan's voice was warning her to back off, but his words were giving her the option. He knew her too well.

To change the subject Shandra said, "Aunt Jo and Uncle Martin are adopting Nelly's daughter, Fawn."

"That's nice. You sure they aren't too old to take it on?" Ryan's tone said he knew she'd changed the subject on purpose.

"Jo has always wanted a daughter. I think it will be good for all of them." She bit down on her bottom lip before saying, "I had thought of doing it."

"Adopting the girl?" The words came out soft and low, thoughtful.

"Yes. We've talked about it."

"We have. Once we're married and feel like we've settled into the whole thing, we can either work on making a family the fun way," his voice dipped into the husky, sexy tone she'd come to love, "or by adoption. Or both. But first we need time to settle in."

"I agree to everything you said." It still amazed her that this man had changed her whole outlook on men and life.

"Do you want to know why I called?" His tone was playful.

"You mean it wasn't to catch me being naughty?" After she blurted it out, she realized she'd acknowledged what she did was wrong.

Ryan laughed. "Gotcha! No, it wasn't to tell you, you were caught with your hand in the cookie jar. I'm coming tomorrow. I switched and got Friday off as well as all next week."

"That's wonderful! We can go to a casino in Omak tomorrow night." Her mind was spinning with the fact they could talk to Duke sooner rather than later.

"Since when have you become a gambler?" he asked.

She laughed. "Not to gamble, to talk with someone who might be a person of interest in Nelly's murder."

"Shandra, what did I just say about the agent assigned to the murder?"

"But he doesn't know about this person. I know because of my connections here." She smiled. People were slowly accepting her as a Higheagle and a family member of the reservation.

"How do you know he doesn't already have this man in his sights and that you'll be stepping into his investigation?" Ryan had dealt with Shandra's hardheadedness enough to know when to push and when to back off. Unfortunately, when it came to the murder of someone she knew, she tended to dig in and not let go.

"Can you find out if he's looking into a Duke Waters?" she asked sweetly.

Ryan laughed. "Now you break the sugar out when you want me to ask a friend to put his job on the line."

"No! I don't want you or your friend to get into trouble. I have a feeling about this guy. We need to talk to him. I'll tell you all the details when you get here."

Ryan made a note of the name and visited with her a few more minutes before hanging up. Dialing his friend's number, he wondered when the friendship card would be filled and Derek would tell him to go fly a kite when he asked for information into cases he shouldn't have any knowledge about.

"Ryan, my man, what's up?" Derek asked, his voice open and warm.

We'll see how long that lasts. "Hey Derek, how's the wife, kids, life?"

His friend rattled on for several minutes and when he'd finished the update said, "I received your wedding invitation. Colville Indian Reservation seems like a strange place for a destination wedding."

Ryan laughed. "It would be if the bride wasn't half Nez Perce."

"Ahhh, and she's up there causing the agent in charge of a murder investigation fits." Derek laughed. "Man, you picked yourself a spitfire. Did you know she picked a lock to get into the crime scene?"

A grin spread across his face even though he'd never let Shandra know he found her spunk and inventiveness hot. "Yeah, I heard that. And as you can guess, I'd like to keep her safe. Any chance you could keep me apprised of who Agent Tremaine is looking at as suspects?"

Derek's side of the conversation went silent.

"Derek, if that's asking one too many favors, I understand."

"I'm back. He has listed a Tripp Talman, seen arguing with the victim, and a Jessie Lawyer, also seen arguing with the victim the night before."

Jessie Lawyer? Why was that name sending up bells?

"Thanks. I'm headed up there tomorrow to keep Shandra in check. I'll make sure she doesn't go busting into Tremaine's case. I owe you another steak dinner."

"Yes, you do."

A thought struck. "You wouldn't happen to have the ME's findings, would you?"

"Stabbing. She figures an eight-inch blade made of

a thick metal. Bruising around the entry has an unusual shape for most knife handles. The person wielding the knife was either lucky or knew what they were doing. ME says the knife went in at an angle to do the most damage."

"And the weapon hasn't been found?" Ryan knew the answer but wanted to make sure.

"No. The agent and a tribal police officer searched the area around the sweat lodge, but haven't come up with one." Derek made the sound of a half laugh. "Sweat Lodge. Didn't know those things were still used."

Ryan wasn't going to tell him he'd been requested by Shandra's Uncle Martin to do a ceremonial sweat with Shandra's male family members. He'd stared down the enemy in Iraq and gang lords in Chicago, but thinking about sitting naked in a dark enclosed area with Shandra's male family members, he was terrified.

"They still hold ceremonial sweats, I guess. That's what Shandra told me. Thanks for the information." Ryan said a few more pleasantries and ended the conversation.

He'd learned two important things. Shandra was on the tail of someone the agent didn't know about and there was a good chance the person who killed Nelly had done it before. He wasn't going to get a lick of sleep tonight. He might as well pack his clothes and head for the reservation.

Chapter Nine

The dogs barked a welcome to someone driving in as Shandra helped her aunt place breakfast on the table. Andy and Uncle Martin were out feeding the horses. They'd greet whoever was visiting.

Fawn shuffled into the kitchen, a teddy bear clutched in one arm and digging at her sleepy eyes with the other hand.

"Good morning, sleepyhead," Shandra said, squeezing the girl's shoulders in a quick hug.

Aunt Jo moved away from the griddle of pancakes and wrapped her arms around the child. "Did you sleep well? We can get more things that will make that room yours."

"Where's momma?" the child asked.

Sorrow filled Jo's eyes as she kissed the top of Fawn's head. "Remember? She was hurt and won't be coming to see you anymore. That's why you are living with us." Jo raised the child's face to peer into her eyes.

Shandra's tears burned her eyeballs. Fawn was so

young to have lost her mother. Too young to fully comprehend what had happened.

"Look what I found lurking around outside," Andy said, swinging the screen door open and walking in.

Shandra glanced over his shoulder and spotted a familiar face. "Ryan! What are you doing here so soon?" Her heart hammered against her ribs. He'd come earlier than she'd thought. Was it to keep her from sticking her nose into things or because he missed her?

"I couldn't sleep, so I started out last night. When I couldn't keep my eyes open I pulled over and slept." He held out an arm and she curled into his embrace.

"I'm happy to see you. Someone needs to keep your bride-to-be focused on what she needs to learn," Aunt Jo said, sending a scolding glance Shandra's direction.

Shandra brushed off her aunt's comment and led Ryan over to Fawn. "Ryan, I'd like you to meet Fawn. Fawn, this man will be my husband in a month, which means you can consider him family, too."

A smile curved on the child's face. "Another uncle?"

Ryan glanced at Shandra.

"I haven't introduced her to any other men. She's talking about her mother's friends." She shifted her attention back to Fawn. "Yes, another uncle, only this one is a real uncle."

"Pleased to meet you, Fawn. Shandra told me what a wonderful little girl you are." Ryan held out his hand and they shook.

Fawn giggled. "I have a Princess pony."

"You'll have to show her to me while I'm here."

Ryan inhaled deeply. "It smells like Aunt Jo's fabulous pancakes are for breakfast." He stood and dropped his duffel bag off his shoulder. "I'll put this upstairs and clean up a bit."

Ryan had barely cleared the room when Aunt Jo waved at Shandra, "Go on. Fawn can help me finish putting things on the table."

Shandra grinned and took the stairs two at a time, bumping into the back of Ryan when he stopped at the top.

"Whoa! What's your hurry?" He pulled her into a hug.

"This."

They stood embracing for several minutes before Ryan released her. "I've learned a few things since we talked."

She followed him into what had been Coop's room and now was the guest room since she visited more than Coop these days. He'd finished college and was working for a technology firm in Spokane. His fiancée, Sandy, had her last year of college to finish and then the two planned to marry.

"What did you learn?" She took a seat on the bed.

"Agent Tremaine isn't looking into the man you mentioned, but he is questioning Tripp Talman—"

"That's the young man I saw Nelly arguing with," Shandra interrupted.

"And Jessie Lawyer. Why is that name familiar?"

"Jessie? I don't understand? Why her?"

Ryan sat on the bed beside her and picked up one of her hands. "Who is she?"

"She's the woman who was infatuated with my dad and sits in the Ketch Pen every day getting drunk. Why her?"

"She'd been seen arguing with the victim the night before her death."

Shandra twisted her head to peer at Ryan. She'd talked with Jessie yesterday and the woman hadn't even remembered who she was. Why would she be arguing with Nelly? Unless she saw Nelly with Duke? He seemed to be Jessie's new infatuation.

"I saw Jessie yesterday. She doesn't seem coherent enough to actually kill anyone." Shandra stood as the smell of the pancakes wafted up the stairs to the room. Her stomach grumbled.

"Where did you see her yesterday?" Ryan tugged on her hand, drawing her attention back to him.

"The Ketch Pen." She could tell by the look in his eyes, he wasn't happy.

"What were you doing there?"

"Velma said that Billy Crow, who practically lives at the bar, would know where to find Duke Waters, the man we're going to talk to at the casino in Omak today." She smiled. "He did know that Duke has been staying at the casino. Some new love interest it sounded like. He didn't go into detail because Jessie started yelling Duke was her man."

"What does this Duke have to do with the murder?" Ryan's stomach grumbled.

"Can we discuss this after breakfast on our way to Omak?" She pulled on his hand, drawing him to his feet. "Since you're here so early we can head to Omak after breakfast."

Ryan groaned. He would never learn how to say no to this woman. And he would always be in fear her dreams and insistence to find murderers would put her in harm. He held her hand and led her back down to the kitchen.

Everyone was seated at the table, their plates piled high with pancakes, even little Fawn. The smile on her face and light in her eyes had to make Jo and Martin feel good. This was the best place for the little girl to grow up.

Even though he was ready to make a family with Shandra, he knew she was still holding back. She didn't believe she'd be a good parent, considering the example she had from her mother and stepfather. But he knew, once she had a child or brought one into their family, she'd be a natural.

He held out Shandra's chair and she sat, bestowing on him the smile he dreamed about seeing every day for the rest of his life. Ryan sat and added pancakes to his plate. When he had them buttered and Jo's homemade syrup drizzling down the sides, he glanced over at Andy. "Did that mare you were worried about last fall foal okay?"

His one question started everyone talking about the family's main income. He'd mentioned to Andy he'd like to give Shandra a wedding gift of a horse and together they had decided on the foal from the horse he'd just mentioned.

"Starfire had a sturdy colt. He will make someone a fine trail horse," Andy said, his voice hovering just below excitement.

Ryan glanced at Shandra who was watching Fawn and gave a slight shake of his head.

Andy understood he'd said too much and started shoveling food into his mouth.

Jo raised an eyebrow. Even though Andy was

excited about the gift, he hadn't told his mother.

To change the subject, Ryan asked, "Have you managed any dancing lessons?"

Shandra's brow wrinkled into a scowl. "I had my first lesson yesterday." She put a hand on his arm. "I'll tell you more about that later."

Her quick shutdown of the topic and her expression, reminded him of when she first started having dreams with her grandmother in them. She'd been uncertain how to explain or tell him about the experiences.

"Another thing to discuss on our way to Omak." He put a bite in his mouth.

"Omak? Why are you going there? Is it to see Duke?" Andy asked.

"We'll have none of that talk here," Jo said, patting Shandra's arm and glancing at Fawn.

~*~

They had barely pulled onto the county road when Ryan started asking questions. Shandra had known that he would want to be told about everything. She filled him in on everyone she'd talked with and what she knew so far.

"I believe Duke has more interest in his daughter than he let Nelly know."

"Why do you think that?" Ryan asked.

"Because someone has been sending money once a month since Fawn was born. When Jo talked to Nelly's grandmother about raising Fawn, Birdie was afraid if she doesn't have the child she won't get the money."

"You believe that Duke is the one sending the money?"

"It's the only person who makes sense. He is the

one who Nelly claims is the father. Why would anyone else send money if that's what she believed." Shandra had thought about this ever since Aunt Jo had told her. "And I believe she was no longer involved with drugs." Shandra wanted to believe that Nelly had stopped helping Duke sell drugs when she was told about the scholarship and how it could get her off of the reservation.

"You know sometimes people get in further than they think, and then they don't know how to get out," Ryan said, reaching over and giving Shandra's hand a squeeze.

"I know. I really think Nelly was trying to make a change. I think that's what got her killed. I don't think it was jealousy. I think it was due to her trying to get out of Duke's business." She didn't think Tripp would have worried about Nelly saying anything to Wendy. Everyone knew Nelly's reputation, and Wendy would have either blown it off or talked it over with Tripp. That was one thing she'd noticed from her visits. While families kept grudges and feuds going with other families, within their own family they made peace. Wendy was the most passive of all of her cousins. She could see her asking Tripp and taking what ever he told her as truth to keep the peace.

That the agent was investigating Jessie Lawyer… She was drunk all the time and couldn't have enacted a plan of revenge from her jealousy. It all rested on Duke and the drugs.

"Now that we've established why we're going to Omak and who we need to question, let's talk about the wedding. That would be a lot more interesting and more pleasurable," Ryan said.

Shandra told him about sensing Grandmother when she danced. That it had surprised, scared, and humbled her that she had fallen into the beat of the drums. She also told him about the Indian rituals she wished to incorporate into the wedding. "And we each will have a purification sweat the night before the wedding." She glanced over.

Ryan had been nodding and making noises to show he was listening. "You mentioned that before. My friend and I sat in his grandfather's sweat lodge when we were about twelve."

"It won't be just you. There will be men from my family who will join you."

He shook his head. "You mean I have to sit naked in a lodge with all of your male relatives? I was thinking just your uncle and maybe your cousins." The way his voice rose an octave she could tell he was nervous.

"You'll be fine, Uncle Martin, Andy, and Coop will be there. They won't let you do anything foolish in front of my other uncles and cousins." She laughed as he made a face at her.

She told him of Velma's offer for Ryan's parents to stay at her house. They had a good laugh over that and continued discussing the wedding the rest of the way to Omak.

~*~

The 12 Tribes Casino was easy to see from the highway. Ryan took a right onto the road leading to the large building sitting out in the middle of sagebrush. The entrance had tall square pillars, taller than the two-story casino. A four-story rectangular hotel was attached to the right of the casino.

This time of day there were only the diehard gamblers pushing buttons, making the machines chime, sing, and shout out. Shandra wasn't sure how they would find Duke. As far as she knew he wasn't a casino owner, it was owned by the tribes. But if this was where he was staying maybe they should have gone to the hotel.

She glanced at Ryan. He would know what to do.

Ryan led her straight to the security guard.

"Hello, we're looking for Duke Waters. Would you have an idea where we could find him?" Ryan asked, smiling at the man as if they were good friends.

The security guard looked them over and asked, "How do you know Duke?"

"We are friends of someone he knows," Shandra said.

The security guard looked them over again, pulled out a phone, and spoke into it. "There's two people here to talk to Duke." He listened to the phone, nodded, and said, "Walk all the way to the back of the casino. You'll see an elevator marked 'employees only,' take that to the second floor."

Shandra didn't wait for the man to ask more questions, she spun around and headed toward the other side of the casino, walking briskly through the red and blue decor. Ryan grabbed her elbow, slowing her down.

He walked beside her and commented, "All casinos have cameras. If Duke is on the second floor of the casino, he has access to the monitors and has already seen us."

At the elevator, Ryan pushed the button with the arrow pointing up. Once inside, he continued, "He might recognize you from your trips and involvement on the reservation. If he's smart enough to recognize you, he most likely also knows you are getting married to a cop. Let me do all the talking. Don't just jump in and say something that we both might regret."

Shandra glanced sideways at Ryan as the elevator dinged and the doors started to open. His face was set in the stoic manner she'd seen many times when they were about to question a witness.

Ryan led her through the open door. They were stopped by an arm the size of a small tree trunk.

"That's as far as you go until I check you out," a man of Native American descent, nearly a head taller than Ryan and twice as broad, said.

She wondered if his family was part of the Colville Tribe. Or if he had come from some other place.

Shandra shifted closer to Ryan.

The man grabbed the strap of her purse, pulling it off her shoulder.

"Hey!" She made a grab for it, but Ryan held her arm.

The big lug shoved his hand inside, rifled around, and came up with her wallet. He opened it, studying her drivers license and then her. He grunted and shoved the wallet back in the purse and handed it to her.

"Turn around." The man motioned with a finger at Ryan.

Ryan faced the wall. The man began patting him as she'd watched Ryan pat down suspects.

Shandra's breathing stopped. Was Ryan packing a gun? He sometimes did when he was off duty and they were questioning people.

She let her breath out, when the man pulled out Ryan's wallet, read his name, and handed it back.

"You're clean," the man said. He led the way down a small hallway to a door. Opening the door, he motioned for them to enter.

Ryan's hand on Shandra's lower back eased her into the room.

A man, she presumed was Duke, sat behind a desk. He had a narrow face, long straight nose, and chin with a dimple. He wore a dress shirt. His gaze scanned the length of her and then bounced over to Ryan, who stood beside her.

The squeak of someone squirming on a chair caught her attention. Two men, she'd guess in their twenties, sat on a couch. They wore jeans, T-shirts, and had rolled bandanas tied around their heads.

"Shandra Higheagle and Ryan Greer," the big man behind them said and closed the door.

Ryan urged her further into the room.

"Shandra Higheagle," Duke said. "You're that do-gooder potter who gave Nelly high ideas."

"It's good to strive for high expectations for oneself," Shandra said.

Duke laughed. "Those aren't good words for young people on a reservation. Gets them thinking they are above their status."

The two on the couch stirred. Duke glanced at them. "You can go. I'll call you when I hear anything."

The two glared at her and Ryan and walked to the door with reluctance. She made sure to capture their faces in her mind, in case they showed up around her family.

When the door closed, with more momentum than was needed, she studied Duke.

"You came looking for me. What did you want?"

he said, returning her gaze. She didn't like the lack of emotion in his dark eyes.

"When was the last time you saw Nelly Bingham?" Ryan asked.

"You say that like you're a cop." Duke narrowed his eyes and starred at Ryan. "You are, aren't you? What the hell you asking me about Nelly for?"

"When was the last time you saw her?" Ryan persisted.

Shandra was glad he'd told her to let him do the talking.

"I don't know. Two, three months ago. She came to me saying how she'd finished her GED and was applying for the scholarship and she didn't want me calling her anymore and asking her to do favors." He glared at Shandra. "That is all your fault. I lost my best clucker because you put it in her head she could do better off the reservation."

"Was she a dowry babe?" Ryan asked.

Shandra stared at him. She had no idea what Duke meant when he called Nelly a clucker. Was it another name for being a chicken? And dowry babe, what was that?

Duke laughed cynically. "She refused to use drugs. Said she wasn't that stupid. But she did just about everything else to try and make me put a ring on her finger."

"Why didn't you? You two have a child," Shandra asked, unable to keep quiet any longer.

Ryan put a hand on her arm, but she held Duke's gaze.

"That isn't my brat. I've told her enough times to quit saying so. I offered a paternity test and she refused." He glanced at Ryan and back to her. "What does that tell you? She knows the brat isn't mine but wants to make me suffer her insinuations."

Shandra wondered if that were true. She couldn't ask Nelly but planned to ask her grandmother.

"You talk as if Nelly is still alive," Ryan said.

His statement shook Shandra as well as Duke. Or Duke was a good actor.

"What do you mean by that?"

"Someone ended her life on Tuesday. Where were you on Tuesday?" Ryan asked.

The man's face went from disbelief to red with rage. "What kind of a question is that?"

"Exactly what it sounds like." Ryan had dealt with this kind before. They used feigned rage to keep from answering the question that would put them behind bars.

"You think I killed her? And who are you coming in here and asking me? I didn't see a badge. You aren't a fed and you aren't tribal police." Duke stood up and pointed to the door. "Get out!"

He must have pressed a button as he stood because the door opened and the refrigerator-sized man who'd frisked him earlier appeared.

"Make sure these two leave the premises," Duke said.

Ryan hustled Shandra out in front of him when she glanced over her shoulder with determination. "Keep going," he whispered in her ear, following the large man to the elevator. The compartment felt half the size with the man in the elevator with them.

At the first floor, he walked beside them to the front of the casino, passing the security guard. The man nodded and didn't say a word. Had he known they wouldn't receive a congenial reception? Ryan made a mental note to have Officer Rider check out the employees of the casino as well as the whereabouts of Duke Waters on Tuesday. He couldn't do anything on the reservation, but he could guide the one tribal policeman who seemed to listen to outsiders.

Chapter Ten

"Can you believe that man?" Shandra said when Ryan had pulled out onto the highway.

"Not a word," Ryan replied. "Call Logan and hand me the phone."

Shandra looked up Logan's number on her phone and hit dial before handing it over to Ryan.

She could hear Logan's voice but not make out what he said by way of greeting.

"Logan, this isn't Shandra, it's Ryan." Ryan listened and said, "Could you do a background check on Duke Waters—"

Ryan nodded. "Yes, I know he's dealing drugs. I want to know where he was on Tuesday."

He listened again. "He lit up like a flare when I asked him where he was. From past experience that means he either had something to do with Nelly's death or had been nearby when she was killed."

Another pause. "Yeah, I want to know why he has an office in the Twelve Tribes Casino and if any of the employees at the casino have prior records."

Ryan rolled his eyes. "Yes, I know the Feds are working on this. But it feels like they're going the wrong direction. If we-you come up with more information in the case, they might switch gears." He nodded and handed the phone back to Shandra. "He wants to talk to you."

She took the phone. "Hi Logan."

"Shandra, you and that man of yours need to be careful. Duke might look dumb, but he is dangerous."

"Don't worry, we know that." She glanced at Ryan. Had they just put targets on their backs for pushing Duke? "Could there be anyone else who fathered Nelly's daughter? Duke says when he asked for a paternity test, she refused to do it."

Logan let out a breath. "That was five years ago. I'll have to think on that. She has always been available for anyone who was interested, if you know what I mean."

She thought of Andy's confession. "Yeah, I know what you mean."

"You might ask Pim Solomon. She and Nelly were friends before they both left school."

"Thanks, I'll do that." She started to close the phone.

"Don't forget your visit to grandmother, she's looking forward to it," Logan reminded her.

"Thank you, with all of this I had forgotten." She slid her finger across the phone.

"What was that about?" Ryan asked, glancing over and then back to the road.

"Logan wanted to make sure that I showed up to visit his grandmother. She's looking forward to it." She grimaced. "And it's today at two."

Ryan glanced at the clock on his dashboard. "We'll have time to eat and you can show me the crime scene before we go to see Logan's grandmother."

She nodded, uncertain if the agent would have someone watching the area since she and Velma had breached the locked gate.

~*~

Ryan could tell by the way Shandra fidgeted she was worried about them checking out the crime scene. "Don't worry, we won't go near it if there is a policeman on guard."

He turned down the road to the community center and into the parking lot.

"Let's walk from here," Shandra said.

He'd planned to suggest the same thing. Less conspicuous to walk, see a police car and turn around, than in a vehicle.

He noticed Jo's car was parked near the community center's entrance. "Does your aunt work here every day?"

Shandra nodded. "She's the Community Coordinator. She has to make sure things are open and ready for groups that use the building, and she books events and makes up the schedules. It keeps her busy."

"Which way?" he asked.

"The road around the side of the building."

He grasped her hand and they followed the road to the back of the building. That's when he spotted the privacy fence and roofs of outbuildings. Studying the enclosure, he noticed what looked like the top of a fair-sized sweat lodge. He didn't see a vehicle in the area. If they had swept the area for evidence, they wouldn't be making it off limits anymore.

"It looks like no one is here," Shandra said, lengthening her strides.

Ryan kept up with her and noted there wasn't a lock on the gate. "Looks like they've finished gathering evidence." He opened the gate and stepped through.

Shandra followed, stopping inside the gate. "Over there." She pointed to a spot not far from the gate. "That's where she was laying. She looked as if she were trying to crawl for help."

Ryan walked toward the area. There were faint darker stains in the dry dirt. He had to agree with Shandra's comment about the victim crawling. There were definite drag lines in the dirt. It surprised him the Feds gathering the evidence hadn't messed them up.

He crouched at what appeared to be where she'd lost her struggle to stay alive and faced the direction the crawl marks pointed. "She came from over there. By the pile of wood." Ryan stood and walked toward the less than a cord of wood stacked to the side of the sweat lodge.

"Who would she have been meeting in here?" he asked.

"According to Moses, young people use this for a place to make out."

He studied Shandra. "Tell their parents they are going to the community center then meet here?" He shook his head. "I guess kids are kids and will use whatever quiet place they can find. But Nelly was a young woman, why would she need to meet anyone here?"

"She lived with her grandmother and daughter." Shandra shrugged.

"But any man she would be with should have a place."

"Unless he were married or wanted their relationship hidden." Shandra stepped up to the blanket covering the sweat lodge. She'd been told this was a sacred place. Sweat lodges were used for purifications and religious reasons. However, if the weapon was in here, it would be more disruptive to the sacredness than her and Ryan looking.

"Do you think the police looked in here?" She ducked in and he followed.

They stood inside the opening a moment, allowing their eyes to get accustomed to the dim lighting.

He took a step to the left.

"This is a sacred space so be respectful of the area as you look," Shandra said, not moving.

"It could also hide evidence," he said, continuing toward what appeared to be the fire pit.

"What kind of evidence?" Shandra's voice came from directly behind him.

"Something left behind by the killer. The murder weapon."

"What was it?" Shandra asked, standing beside him, staring at the pit.

"A long, wide bladed knife." He felt along the sides of the pit, sticking his fingers in the crevices between the rocks. "The coroner said the bruising from the handle made a mark that reminded her of the base of an antler."

Shandra straightened and stared at Ryan. The last time she'd visited, Wendy had shown her all the regalia she'd made for powwows and traditional ceremonies. She'd been proud of several knives with antler handles.

Taking a deep breath and letting it out slowly to slow down her racing heart that feared her cousin had committed this crime, she grasped Ryan's sleeve. "Wendy makes knives like that."

He stopped searching and faced her. "What are you talking about?"

"I told you Wendy and Tripp are dating. Tripp said he was breaking it off with Nelly, but she wanted him to come to Spokane with her." She swallowed and added, "And Wendy was missing around the time Nelly was murdered."

"Was she carrying anything that could conceal a knife?"

Shandra thought about the day. "She had the doeskin for my dress wrapped up in a blanket, but she didn't take it with her to the restroom." What had Wendy been wearing? Jeans, shirt, and vest. "I don't remember her having anything that would have allowed her to carry a knife around, but she could have hidden it before entering the center or left it in Velma's car."

"We need to have a talk with your cousin." Ryan did a quick circle of the fire pit, looked into the crannies of the sweat lodge and led her out.

"We have to see Logan's grandmother first. It's almost two." Shandra had hoped her visit with Mrs. Rider would have been while she was calm and focused only on her upcoming wedding. Now she had so many things bouncing around inside her head, she hoped she was a good guest for the old woman.

Chapter Eleven

Following Aunt Jo's directions, Shandra directed Ryan to a small house on the edge of Nespelem. The yard was tidy with a peony bush on each side of the door and iris and bleeding-hearts blooming in the flower bed the width of the house. The colors gave the gray house a cheerier appearance.

"Do you want me to come in?" Ryan asked.

"I'm sure she wouldn't mind. We're going to talk mostly about grandmother. Mrs. Rider and my grandmother were best friends from childhood." She smiled. Finally, she would get to visit with someone who knew her grandmother in a capacity other than family.

Ryan glanced at his phone. "I'll just stay out here and make some phone calls. When you're finished, we'll go see Wendy."

"Okay." She opened the door.

Ryan caught her hand. "Forget about the murder and enjoy your time with your grandmother's friend."

She peered into his eyes. He knew her yearning to learn more about her grandmother. "I'll try."

He released her hand and she slid out of the truck. "Do you want me to call you when I'm done?"

"I'll be right here." He pulled his work pack out of the back seat. "I'll be looking people up on my computer."

"You aren't getting paid to solve this murder," she said.

"It's not about the money. It's about finding the truth."

She blew him a kiss. "That's what I love about you." Shandra spun around and walked up the narrow dirt path to the front door.

The door opened before she could knock.

A woman of average height, a little overweight, and a wizened face smiled at her. "Shandra! So good to see you." She opened the door farther and spotted the pickup. "Your man can come in, too."

"He's catching up on work. But he'd love to meet you when we finish talking." Shandra stepped over the threshold, inhaling sage and fresh baked cookies. The living room held two chairs and a small couch. A flat screen tv hung on the wall.

"Logan gave me that for Christmas last year. Such a good boy. He said my living room was too crowded with the old tv that took up that whole corner." She pointed to a corner that sported a winding staircase plant stand. "Your Aunt Jo gave me the plant stand. So thoughtful."

She led Shandra through the living room and into the kitchen. It was painted a cheery yellow with Indian sun drawings on the towels and cabinets.

"I made tea and cookies." Mrs. Rider motioned for Shandra to sit at the table facing the sliding glass door that led out to a small patio. The backyard had a small patch of grass, a small garden, and a flower bed that was blooming.

"It appears you have a way with plants," Shandra said as the woman placed a cup of tea in front of her.

"I've always loved the feel of dirt in my hands and growing things. I'm not sure what my ancestors would think of that." She laughed. "We were a semi-nomadic tribe, moving from place to place to harvest the foods as they were ready. We didn't stay in one place and grow our food. We collected what the creator had provided for us." Mrs. Rider placed a plate of cookies on the table and sat.

"You have the same look as your grandmother at your age. If I had come upon you on a street, I would have known who you were." Mrs. Rider reached across the table with an outstretched hand.

Shandra grasped her long fingers and thin hand. "I've had others I've met on the reservation mistake me for grandmother." The connection of their hands sent a calm over Shandra. She no longer felt the urgent need to think about Nelly. She wanted to know more about the past and her grandmother.

"Your grandmother would be proud of the woman you've become." Mrs. Rider pulled her hand back and picked up a cookie. "She always told me you would be the one to carry on her work."

Shandra sat back. "What did she mean by that? Grandmother was a healer and an elder of the Seven Drums. I am neither." She thought a minute. "Nor do I plan to be either."

The older woman smiled. Her eyes lit with a knowing gleam. "She meant the dreams. Finding the truth through your dreams."

Shandra shook her head. "That's only because grandmother shows me."

"If you didn't believe, you wouldn't have the dreams." Mrs. Rider picked up her tea cup and sipped.

"Tell me about Grandmother." Shandra didn't want to ponder what the woman had said about her carrying on a family tradition. She wanted to learn about the woman she'd been scared to come see.

"Minnie was a beauty. She could have married any man on the reservation. Any man who saw her asked her. But she had eyes for your grandfather from the time she was a small girl. We saw him at a powwow. She elbowed me as we were waiting for the procession to start. 'Look at that boy,' she said. 'I'm going to marry him.' I laughed and asked her why she was thinking about marrying at our young age. By the end of the powwow, they had exchanged names and addresses." Mrs. Rider shook her head. "Those two wrote to each other once a week and met at all the ceremonies, powwows, and events they could. When Minnie was old enough to marry and the other men came calling, she was polite but to the point. She wasn't marrying until she'd learned all she could about healing. Your grandfather worked with his father at the ranch until Minnie was ready to marry. Afterwards they moved to the ranch, and I never saw a happier couple." Her eyes grew sad. "It tore your grandmother up when she couldn't cure your grandfather. Then she lost your father." The woman mumbled words Shandra didn't understand.

"And she lost me." Shandra's heart ached for the woman she'd only recently come to hold in her heart.

Mrs. Rider shook her head. "Minnie told me over and over again, you would come back." She smiled. "As always, Minnie was right."

"I only remember parts of the summer I spent with her. It was my anger at my mom and stepfather that brought me here. It was one of the best times in my life, once I got over my anger and realized I was loved and wanted." She sighed. "But it took Ella's death to make me realize I'd been staying away for fear everyone would hate me for not coming back sooner."

"Minnie told your family and me that you would come when the time was right." She patted Shandra's hand. "And here you are. Getting married in the traditional way and helping others on the reservation."

That reminded Shandra of Nelly. "I'm too late to help one person."

"Don't worry over her. She had set her future years ago when she took up with Duke Waters. She was old enough and wise enough to know what that man did."

"But when the heart is involved and you are young, you don't always think clearly." She thought of her first infatuation. Her college professor who'd pulled her into his web of cruel, sadistic love. Or what she'd thought at the time was love and learned afterwards wasn't. She'd been strong enough to get away. That was why she'd felt a kinship with Nelly. Shandra had believed the young woman was ready to get away from her oppressor. Now, she wasn't so sure.

Mrs. Rider nodded. "That is true. The heart can make the mind think they are right when they are doing wrong. But in Nelly's case, I believe it was more her proving her power over others."

This caught her attention. "What do you mean by that?"

"Nelly's mother walked out on her and her father when Nelly was less than a year old. That's why she was living with Birdie. Then her father used drugs and overdosed, which is why she never touched the stuff."

"Yet she worked for Duke, bringing him customers. Why would she do that, after what happened to her father?" Shandra was beginning to think she hadn't known the young woman as well as she'd thought.

"Ahhh, but she fell for Duke. The older man. Old enough to be a father figure. And he played her emotions, used her as he needed by keeping her thinking he loved her."

Shandra could see the man she'd met this morning doing just that. He'd had a cold heart. She'd witnessed it in his eyes. Why hadn't Nelly seen through that? "Do you believe Duke is the father of her baby?"

The old woman shook her head. "I'm not sure. Your grandmother had an idea but she didn't tell me. I do know that Nelly was sleeping with more than Duke back then. She was the talk at many of the gatherings because she didn't care if a man had a wife or girlfriend. She did whatever it took to get a man or woman buying from Duke. It was as if she thought by bringing him business, he'd love her more. The people who were clean and wanted to keep their significant others and children clean would avoid Nelly." She shook her head. "It's sad. Because in the end, all Nelly wanted was to be accepted. She just didn't know how to do that."

Shandra thought about the conversations she'd had with the young woman on previous visits. She had seemed open to having Shandra as a friend. Someone who didn't know her past or judge her.

"Do you have any idea of how I could find out who she slept with five years ago?" Shandra picked up her tea cup.

"Why are you so interested?"

"Aunt Jo and Uncle Martin have taken in Fawn, Nelly's daughter. I'd like to know who the father is and make sure he won't come along after Jo has become attached and want to take the child away." She wasn't going to add that someone had been paying Birdie money once a month since the child's birth.

"Your aunt has a heart of gold. One day it will do her in. I hope it isn't over this child." Mrs. Rider waved a hand. "I have a letter for you. Your grandmother left it with me to give to you when she passed. Wait here while I get it."

Shandra stared at the woman's back as she left the room. What were you thinking Ella? She drank the rest of her tea and texted Ryan to come in any time. She had a feeling once she read the letter, she would need time to herself to think.

Before the woman returned, Ryan knocked on the door. Shandra started toward the living room, but Mrs. Rider was already at the door.

"Come in. You must be Ryan, Shandra's young man." The older woman took Ryan's arm and led him to the kitchen. "Have a seat." When he was seated, she placed a cup in front of him and filled all the tea cups.

Shandra sat, her gaze on the woman, wondering what she had done with the letter.

At that moment, the older woman placed an envelope on the table beside her tea cup. "Tell me what you think of our reservation?" she asked Ryan.

Shandra barely heard Ryan's response as she stared at the envelope. What could grandmother have written to her before her death?

"Shandra? Shandra," Ryan said, drawing her thoughts from the missive to him.

"Yes?"

"Mrs. Rider asked about the wedding. You know more about that than I do." Ryan studied her. He knew something was off.

"Plans are to have the ceremony at the Powwow grounds. Family will bring food for afterwards."

The older woman nodded. "I like that. Traditional." She glanced at Ryan. "Are you wearing buckskins? I heard Wendy is making Shandra a traditional doeskin dress."

"No, I'm going to stay true to my roots. Jeans, boots, cowboy hat, and cowboy cut jacket."

Shandra put a hand on Ryan's arm. "He's handsome in his fancy clothes."

"I can tell you are a lucky woman." Mrs. Rider smiled and peered at Ryan. "Logan also believes you are a lucky man."

"That I am," Ryan said, patting Shandra's hand still resting on his arm. "I'm sorry to take her away, but we still have a lot to accomplish and we only have until Sunday to get it done."

"I understand."

Shandra's gaze shot to the envelope now under the woman's hand. Ryan must have felt her anxiety because he stood, studying her.

"Thank you for the tea and the stories about Grandmother," she said, standing.

"You're welcome. Come by any time." Mrs. Rider stood, picking up the letter at the same time.

They walked through the living room to the door.

Ryan opened the door and stepped out.

Mrs. Rider pulled Shandra into a hug and whispered, "May the Creator look over you." The old woman released her and held out the envelope.

Chapter Twelve

Ryan stood three feet from the door, waiting for Shandra to exit the house. She strode out, past him, and into his truck before he had time to catch up to her.

He opened the passenger door and noticed the envelope in her hands. "What's that?"

Her gaze didn't leave the object. "Grandmother left it with Mrs. Rider to give to me." Her head swiveled and she peered into his eyes. "I don't know whether to open it, keep it and read later, or never open it."

He put his hands over hers. "If your grandmother wanted you to have the letter, then you need to open it."

She nodded. "But not here. At the ranch." She slid the envelope into her purse.

"Do you want to go straight there or talk to your cousin?"

"Let's see Wendy. The letter has kept this long, it can wait." She pulled on her seatbelt and latched it.

"You're the boss," he said, kissing her lightly on the lips and heading to the driver's side of the pickup.

She directed him to her Aunt Velma's house. It was on the opposite side of Nespelem and had some acreage. A large barn stood behind the house.

"Wendy works on her projects in a section of the barn." Shandra was unbuckled and her door opening before he had the vehicle in park.

"Whoa. Slow down." He captured her arm before she slid off the seat. "Are you sure you don't want to read that letter?"

Her gaze landed everywhere but her purse. "No. It can wait. We're here and there's no sense in missing a chance to ask Wendy questions."

"Take a deep breath and wait for me to come to your side of the pickup." He pocketed the keys and made his way around to the passenger side. "See that didn't hurt to just sit there and relax."

He grasped her hand, drew her out of the vehicle, and closed the door. "House or barn?"

"If we go to the house first, and Velma is there, she'll follow us to the barn. Better try the barn and hope we only find Wendy and Velma didn't see us drive up." Shandra led him along the side of the house and out to the barn.

They entered through a man door beside two larger doors.

The smell of leather in all stages of tanning caught him off guard. He knew her cousin made traditional regalia for powwow dancers but hadn't realized she did the full process.

He'd yet to meet this cousin and presumed it was the young woman leaning over a table that hit her above her waist. She pulled leather lacing through a garment.

"Hi Wendy," Shandra said.

Wendy jumped, stared at them, then smiled timidly. "You startled me. Mother makes so much noise when she comes in I don't think about anyone else sneaking up on me."

Her cheeks blossomed a rosy color as she stepped out from behind the table. "If you're Ryan, you can't see what is on the table."

"I am." He held out his hand. They shook, and she drew him back toward the door.

"I'm working on Shandra's dress." Wendy nodded back to the table. "It's bad luck for you to see her dress."

"Does that hold true for your culture?" he asked.

She shook her head. "No, but you are honoring both cultures."

"We are. I'm so happy you are working on my dress." Shandra bestowed a smile that lit up her eyes and made his heart thump hard against his rib cage. It was the same smile that had concreted his notion he was falling in love with her.

"It's a pleasure to make a dress that will not only be part of a wedding ceremony but will be kept in our family." Wendy waved to half a dozen folding chairs leaning up against the wall. "Are you staying long enough to sit?"

"We are," Shandra said.

Ryan took the hint and brought two chairs over. He unfolded them, and Wendy wiped the dust off as he grabbed a third chair. He glanced at the shelf above the chairs. Three antler-handled knives lay on the shelf. The blades shone like freshly honed steel. The handles were polished to a shine. He wondered if the hilt on one of them would match the bruising around the stab wound on the victim.

When they were all seated, Wendy glanced from one to the other. "Why did you come to see me? Have you decided to add more traditional clothing?" Her gaze landed on him.

"No, we have some questions for you." Shandra faced her cousin. "I saw Tripp and Nelly arguing at the Community Center the morning she died. At the time I didn't know it was her. Not until later when I saw the clothing she wore. But then later, when you left Aunt Jo's office to go to the restroom, you were gone a long time. I went to wash my hands and you weren't in the restroom. But I did see two people making out in Tripp's pickup." Shandra drew in a deep breath and said, "Did you see Tripp and Nelly in the pickup?"

Ryan knew it was hard for Shandra to see any of her family as a murderer. But he'd learned from all his years in law enforcement, the quiet ones were usually the most methodical when they killed.

Wendy laughed softly. "It wasn't Nelly in the pickup with Tripp. It was me. When I came out of the restroom, he was walking toward the center. I met him, and we went to his pickup." She blushed. "We don't get many chances alone. My mother prefers her daughter be what other daughters are held up to."

Ryan could see she didn't like being the perfect daughter. Could that be why she crafted weapons under the guise of regalia? "Did you and Tripp talk about anything?"

"Nelly. He told me she'd asked him to go to Spokane with her. Like he'd leave drumming and me to follow her." There was fire in her eyes. She didn't like the idea of Nelly taking her man.

"Did he leave when you went back in the building?" Ryan asked, watching her.

"Yes." She didn't flinch.

"And you? Did you go straight into the building?" He saw her flick a gaze Shandra's direction.

"I talked to Pim. Pim Solomon. She was coming out of the center."

"What did she have to say?" Shandra jumped in.

Ryan studied his fiancée. She was interested in this Pim girl. Why?

"Not much. Said she'd heard you were giving out the scholarship but when she'd popped in no one had mentioned she'd received it." Wendy picked at the seam of her jeans. "She seemed as if she wanted to say more, but I wasn't in the mood to talk to her. Not after hearing what Nelly had said to Tripp and knowing you were giving the scholarship to her. I'd hoped the scholarship would get Nelly away from him." She glanced at Ryan. "Pim and Tripp went out a time or two back in high school before she had to leave for a year."

He nodded. It seemed Tripp had a lot of girls in his past. He wondered how many boys Wendy had dated. She seemed out of her league with a player like Tripp. "Did you see where Pim went?"

"No. I just hurried into the center and started measuring Shandra."

Shandra nodded. "That's when Moses came into the office and said he'd found Nelly."

"Can you think of anyone who would hate Nelly enough to kill her?" he asked, knowing she'd probably come up with half a dozen names.

"Not really. Everyone pretty much felt sorry for her. Well, those of us who saw how pathetic she was,"

Wendy said.

"What about all the girlfriends and wives of the men she'd slept with?" Ryan had his money on Duke, but he'd learned a long time ago, you didn't leave any question unanswered or suspect unturned.

"Most of them realized in the end that if their man was dumb enough to sleep with Nelly, he deserved her and left him. In a way, she made it easier for women to find a good man." Wendy frowned.

What she'd said must have sunk in. Tripp had slept with Nelly multiple times from what he could figure.

"Then maybe you should be looking for another boyfriend?" Shandra said softly.

Wendy's eyes widened. "He said that was all before he started going out with me and realized he wanted better. Wanted a good future."

"I hope that's true for your sake," Shandra said, glancing at Ryan.

The door opened and Velma stood in the doorway. "What are you doing huddled up out here? Come in the house for tea."

"Thank you for the invite, Velma, but we need to get back to the ranch." Shandra stood. She didn't want to explain to her aunt why she and Ryan were talking to Wendy alone in the barn.

The large woman frowned. "Why did you come in here and talk to Wendy and not stop by the house?"

"Because we are running behind and had a couple of questions for Wendy," Ryan said, grasping Shandra's hand.

She smiled at him and stood. "I'll come by and see you before we leave Sunday."

"Sunday? You can't leave until we know who

killed Nelly and you pick another scholarship winner." Velma put her hands on her hips and remained blocking the doorway.

"Haven't you called Pim and told her she's the scholarship recipient?" Shandra would have thought her aunt had called as soon as she knew Nelly wouldn't be receiving it. After all, the young woman was Velma's pick.

Velma's stance slacked. "I'm thinking she shouldn't have it."

This shocked Shandra. "Why?"

"Because I didn't like her showing up at the day and time we were going to give the scholarship to someone else. Someone who didn't show because they were dead." Velma shivered. "Seems off."

"I agree." Shandra tugged on Ryan's hand, leading him over to the door. "I think we should go talk to Pim. Where does she live?"

Velma gave them directions to the Solomon house.

As they were parking in the driveway behind three vehicles on blocks and two with broken windows and smashed bodies, Ryan's phone rang.

Shandra opened her door and Ryan grabbed her wrist, keeping her in the vehicle as he carried on the conversation. From his side, she gathered he was talking to someone about the evidence gathered at the crime scene.

She waited, noting there seemed to be no activity happening in the house. The curtains were open, and she hadn't seen anyone moving about.

"Thanks. I'm going to owe you a favor or two after this." He shoved his phone into the holster on his belt and studied the house.

"What did whoever that was have to say?" She was interested in all the facts they could find.

"As we suspected, she didn't die right away. They found traces of hair on her clothing that wasn't hers. It's being checked for DNA. They did check the sweat lodge and found candy wrappers, beer bottles, and residue from drugs. Checking those for prints and DNA. Interesting fact. They didn't find evidence of any vehicle tracks but lots of footprints, coming and going. Two sets from the back of the center, gymnasium area."

"Were there return tracks?" Shandra asked, wondering if the killer had lured Nelly to the sweat lodge then arrived and killed her.

"No return tracks. Whoever walked to the area from the gym didn't return the same way." Ryan nodded to the house. "No one's moved inside the whole time we've sat here. There may not be anyone home."

"We won't know until we try." Shandra stepped out and waited for Ryan to join her before walking up to the bare wood door.

He knocked and they waited.

He knocked again.

"There's no one here." Ryan turned to walk back to the pickup.

Shandra stopped. "There's a sound."

Chapter Thirteen

A soft rumbling sound could be heard behind the door. Shandra remembered Pim had left school for a year to help with her mother. Was Mrs. Solomon an invalid?

The door opened. A woman close to forty sat in a wheelchair, her hand looped through a rope attached to the door. "What do you want?" she asked.

"I'm Shandra Higheagle—"

"Oh my! Come in! Is this about the scholarship?" The woman pulled her bent hand from the loop and used it to push a toggle on the arm of the wheelchair.

Shandra glanced at Ryan. They stepped over the threshold and he closed the door behind them.

"I was hoping to speak with Pim," Shandra said, taking the spot on the couch the woman motioned to.

Ryan stood, leaning a shoulder against the wall beside Shandra.

"Pim is at work. She's a good girl who works hard." The woman smiled. Only one side of her face worked.

"I thought she was doing YSEP today?" Shandra wondered if she'd remembered the right acronym.

"Is today Friday?"

"Yes," Ryan said.

The woman looked flustered. "Then she is at the community center with YSEP." She glanced at the clock. "She should come home any time, now."

"Where does she work the rest of the week?" Shandra asked. The young woman had used her lunch hour to show up at the community center the day Nelly was killed.

"She's been working at the new government center. This week she was in the legal services." Mrs. Solomon peered at her. "My Pim is not a slacker. She always works hard. Didn't she make up the year she had to take off to help me?"

"I heard Pim and Nelly were friends when they both went to school." Shandra noticed the woman grimace even though half of her face remained slack.

"They were friends until Nelly started hanging around with Duke Waters. He's no good. Pim and I both told Nelly to stay away from him." She moved her head in two short twists. "When she tried to get Pim to help her, my Pim told her no and stayed away."

"Pim ever say if she knew who Fawn's father was?" Ryan asked.

The woman glared at him. "Pim wouldn't know. She's a good girl." She acted as if she were trying to spit. "Wendy Wilbur is not such a good girl." As if she remembered who Shandra was, she placed half a smile on her face. "Pim doesn't regard my feelings for others."

Shandra had heard enough. She wanted to find Pim and thought she had an idea of how to make sure she did. "Thank you for your time, Mrs. Solomon." She stood.

Ryan was at the door before she stepped that direction.

"I thought you wanted to talk to Pim?" the woman asked.

"We will another time." Shandra hurried out the door Ryan held open and pulled her phone from her purse.

"Who are you calling?" he asked, catching up to her at the pickup.

"Jo, to hold Pim, if both of them are still there. Then Liz. If Pim is working in the legal department, Liz should be able to track down what she did on Tuesday."

Shandra called Jo. She was getting ready to leave the community center but agreed to look for Pim and keep her in her office until Shandra arrived.

As Ryan drove them to the community center, Shandra dialed the work number she had for Liz.

"Confederated Tribes Legal Aid," a young woman answered the phone.

Shandra shifted her attention to the young woman on the phone. "Is Liz Piney in?"

"Who's calling please?"

"Her cousin, Shandra."

"I'll put your call through."

A few clicks and Liz answered. "Hello, Shandra? What are you calling me for? Word in the family is you are here learning about our traditions."

"I am. But I'm also a bit caught up in the Nelly Bingham murder."

Liz groaned. "Are you getting on the bad side of the Feds again?"

Shandra laughed. "Not yet. Mrs. Solomon said Pim was working YSEP for the legal department this week."

"She'll be here next week, too. Why are you interested in Pim?"

Shandra heard the squeak of a chair in the background. "She was friends with Nelly in school. They might have remained friends without others realizing. And she showed up strangely at the community center Tuesday when we were waiting for Nelly to arrive to receive my scholarship. Aunt Jo was confused by the reason for Pim showing up. I wondered if you could find someone there who Pim might have confided in and find out what time she left for lunch and came back on Tuesday."

Liz gave a whistle. "I'd almost think you believe Pim killed Nelly with all the questions you want answered."

"As far as I can tell, Pim didn't have a reason to kill Nelly but she might have the information we need to prove who did." Shandra had a strong feeling the murder had to do with Fawn. And from her calculations, Pim and Nelly would have still been friends when Nelly became pregnant.

"I'll ask around. And see you at the big party on Saturday."

"What big party?"

The phone went silent.

"Party?" Ryan asked, parking in the Community Center lot.

"I don't know. Liz said she'd see me at the big party on Saturday." She scanned the parking lot. Aunt

Jo's car was in its usual place.

They exited the pickup and strode to the building. She knew Aunt Jo would want to get home and check on Fawn.

Inside the center, she led Ryan to Jo's office. She found Jo talking with Pim.

"Miss Higheagle." Pim shot to her feet.

"Hi Pim. This is my fiancé, Ryan." Shandra motioned to Ryan.

"Pim," he said, leaning his backside on Aunt Jo's desk.

"Can I head home now?" Aunt Jo asked.

"Yes. And thank you." Shandra gave her aunt a brief hug and motioned for Pim to sit back down.

"I don't understand? Mrs. Elwood didn't say you were coming to see me." Pim frowned and glanced from Shandra to Ryan.

"That's because I asked her not to." Shandra took the chair her aunt had vacated.

"Does this have anything to do with the scholarship?" Pim's eyes brightened and her voice rose in excitement.

"Yes and no. I have some questions I'd like answered."

"Sure." The young woman settled back in the chair and smiled at Shandra.

"You and Nelly were friends before she dropped out of school to have Fawn, right?" Shandra studied the woman. The happiness disappeared, replaced by suspicion.

"Yeah. Why do you want to know about Nelly and me?"

"I want to know if she told you who Fawn's father

is." Shandra hoped the young woman could answer that question.

Pim's eyes flashed with anger before her lashes lowered, hiding her emotions. She picked at the hem of her shirt. "She wasn't sure but told everyone it was Duke Waters. She had a thing for the pervie old man."

"Do you believe the father is Duke?" Shandra asked.

Pim shrugged. "I don't know. She'd been sleeping with several boys at the time, getting them to use and start buying from Duke. Honestly, it could have been any of them."

"Can you give me their names?" Shandra glanced at Ryan. He nodded. He'd make note of the names.

"Arthur Randal, Billy Crow, Jeremy Ten, David Forth, just about any high school and adult male. I can't remember all of them." Pim stared her in the eyes. "Nelly was a whore and used people."

The hatred in Pim's eyes startled Shandra. She'd hoped for answers, but the young woman was adding herself to the suspect list. She had a thought.

"Did Nelly and Tripp hook up back then?"

Sparks snapped in the depths of Pim's eyes. "She stole him from me. If she hadn't used her whoring on him, we'd be married. But once she touched him, there was no way my family would ever allow me to marry him." She glared at Ryan and then Shandra. "I'm surprised Velma hasn't done something to spare her sweet Wendy from Tripp's charm." She smirked. "Believe me, he can charm the pants off any woman."

"Why did you really come here Tuesday?" Shandra asked, changing the subject and making a mental note to have a talk with Wendy.

Pim sat up straighter. "I came to look at the list of volunteer jobs for the powwow in July."

Shandra shook her head. "That's not what you said on Tuesday. You asked Jo where the YSEP meeting was going to be held today."

Caught in her lie, her mouth opened slowly and snapped shut. Her gaze flicked between Shandra and Ryan. "I'd heard there would be an announcement Tuesday about the scholarship recipient. When I didn't get called, I thought I'd come by, see if anyone said anything. My mom and I are really hoping for the scholarship. With her medical condition there isn't any way I can go to school without help."

"Did you see Nelly when you arrived?" Ryan asked. He'd let Shandra lead the questions up till now. He had a feeling this young woman knew more about Fawn's father than she let on and she was trying to play on Shandra's sympathies. He was immune after all the years he'd worked as a cop.

Pim's face swung toward him. "No. Why would I? She never showed up."

"I think she was here. I'd witnessed her arguing with Tripp earlier," Shandra said.

At Shandra's statement Pim's eyebrows rose. "She was arguing with Tripp? Here? Wendy was here. Did she see it?"

"No, she didn't know about the argument. But you talked to Wendy," Ryan said, bringing the woman's attention back to him.

She narrowed her eyes. "How do you know?"

"She told us." Ryan tipped his head toward Shandra and she nodded.

"Then you know what we said." Pim crossed her

arms.

"Tell us what you said. We only have Wendy's account." Ryan saw her thinking behind her steady gaze. Either she was bringing up the conversation or figuring what to say that might have been close to what Wendy had said.

"I think I said something about the scholarship. She said Nelly was late to get it. I asked about Tripp. She said they were happy. And I left. She seemed to be distracted." Pim nodded as if she'd just finished a long recitation.

"Wendy told you Nelly was late to receive the scholarship?" Ryan didn't remember Wendy saying if she'd mentioned the scholarship to Pim.

"Yes. She said something like, 'you'd think she'd be on time for her ticket out of here.'" The young woman smiled. "I sure would have been here early."

Ryan was getting mixed conversations from the two young women who had a grudge against the victim. They both had reason to want Nelly out of their way. He could see Pim stabbing her adversary to get what she wanted. While Wendy was practically family and she seemed a bit meek to shove a knife in anyone's belly, even one who was trying to take her boyfriend.

"You have no idea who Fawn's father is?" Shandra asked, making him wonder what she had picked up on that he hadn't.

"I told you. Nelly was sleeping with anyone she could lure into drugs. For all I know it's one of the four who overdosed and are laying in the cemetery." Pim stood. "I'm going home. Mom needs her medication."

Ryan watched the young woman walk out of the office. He glanced down at Shandra. "She just gave us more suspects. If Nelly started four men on drugs who overdosed, they might have some family who were out for revenge."

Shandra nodded and stood. "The more we dig, the more people we find who might have a reason." She sighed. "Including Wendy."

Chapter Fourteen

The Elwood family and their newest addition sat at
the kitchen table waiting for dinner when Shandra
walked through the door with Ryan.

She and Ryan had agreed on the way to the house
not to mention questioning Wendy. Shandra avoided
her aunt's questions about Pim by saying, "What is the
big party happening tomorrow?"

Jo put her hands up as if surrendering. "I had
nothing to do with it. Your Aunt Velma thought you
two needed to see a proper drum ceremony. She invited
everyone in the family, and the seven drums
community, here tomorrow evening for a traditional
fish dinner and thank you dance."

"We're cutting wood for the fire in the morning."
Andy motioned to his father. "You're welcome to
help," he added, smiling at Ryan.

"I wouldn't mind helping out," Ryan glanced at
Shandra. "What will Shandra learn to do?"

"Prepare the food," Andy said.

"And practice her dancing in the evening," Aunt Jo added.

"This sounds like fun. A hands-on look at my heritage." Shandra was happy Velma had come up with the idea. It would also mean Wendy and Tripp would be here. She had more questions for them. "How many people do you think will attend?"

Uncle Martin glanced at his wife. "A hundred or more. Some come to get free food, others come out of curiosity. And the family is not small."

Shandra stared at Ryan. A hundred or more people at the ranch. She had hoped it would be more like fifty. "That's a lot of people! Will we have enough food?"

Aunt Jo patted her arm. "Velma will have gathered donations from family. There will be enough. She has been planning this ever since I told her you were coming."

Shaking her head, Shandra said, "That woman can keep a secret like one hundred people coming to a dinner and ceremony but can't keep secrets that could do her harm?"

Aunt Jo's laugh turned serious. "What has she been saying now?"

"Nothing. I meant the times she and I have questioned people. She doesn't give anyone any slack." Shandra glanced at Ryan. Except her daughter. There were things Pim had said that Shandra wanted clarified, but she didn't feel Aunt Jo was the one to answer her questions.

The timer went off.

"Dinner is ready." Aunt Jo popped out of her chair and headed to the oven.

Andy moved to the refrigerator and placed a plate of carrots and celery on the table and poured milk for himself and Fawn.

When dinner and the dishes were done, she would corner her cousin. He would be the one most likely to tell her the truth. And she still needed to read the letter from Grandmother.

~*~

Ryan sat in one of the chairs circled around an outdoor firepit in the Elwood's backyard. It hadn't occurred to him when he set out to make sure Shandra stayed out of the murder investigation that he would end up just as deep in it. There were so many unanswered questions.

From the banging of dishes and the murmur of voices as Shandra and Jo did the dishes, he knew it would be a while longer before Shandra joined him.

Andy arrived with an armload of wood. "Want me to start a fire?"

"Don't start it on my account, I'm content to listen to the birds and insects." Ryan raised his glass of iced tea to the darkening sky.

"You want a beer?" the young man asked.

"No, I'm good." Ryan studied Andy. Shandra thought a lot of her cousins. From what he'd witnessed so far, she had good reason to be proud of them. "Will there be drinking tomorrow night?"

Andy dropped into a chair across from him. "Only if people bring it. We don't offer it to anyone when there is a celebration here. They get crazy and everyone thinks they are a cowboy, jumping on the horses or going in the pastures and whooping and chasing them." He shook his head, scowling.

"I can see where that would be a problem." He wasn't sure how to phrase his next question. "I know this will be a ceremony more to show Shandra and I what one is like, but do some people come to use it as a place to hook-up?"

Andy's face reddened. "There are some that do. They are also the ones who usually bring the booze."

The next question would be even touchier. "Does Tripp drink?"

"Tripp? Not if he's drumming. And you better believe Aunt Velma will have him drumming to keep him away from Wendy."

Ryan grinned. "I've been trying to decide if Velma likes Tripp dating Wendy, or not."

"She doesn't." Andy kicked at the rock fire pit. "If she had her way, she'd lock Wendy in the barn and not allow her out until Aunt Velma picked her the perfect husband."

"Why does she allow Wendy to date Tripp?" Ryan would have thought the Velma so many feared would have chased Tripp away by now.

"Because Tripp has become interested in tradition. He's learned to play drums, become a Seven Drums follower, and shows Wendy respect." Andy shrugged. "Tripp has dated a lot of girls, but he does act different around Wendy."

"I learned today he was dating Pim Solomon and Nelly took him away from her. You know anything about that?" Ryan finished off his tea and set the glass on the ground beside his chair.

Andy shook his head. "Coop and Sandy would know more about that because Tripp is their age. They'd know more about Tripp's love life. I just know rumors, no facts." He kicked at the rock again with the toe of his cowboy boot. "They'll be here tomorrow night. Velma made them promise."

"Coop and Sandy?" He hadn't seen the two since Shandra and he proved Coop didn't kill Arthur Randal. The name echoed in his head.

"Pim said one of the boys Nelly slept with to start him buying from Duke was Arthur Randal. Does that sound right?"

Andy shrugged. "We know Arthur was selling, but Nelly hated Arthur for banging her around. I can't see her sleeping with him, unless that's when it happened."

Shandra and Martin wandered out to the fire pit.

Ryan pulled a chair closer to his and Shandra sat down.

Martin took the chair next to Andy. "What are you two talking about so intently?"

The younger man shot Ryan a "this is between us" look.

"I was asking Andy what to expect tomorrow night." Ryan put a hand palm up on the arm of Shandra's chair. She pressed her palm against his and he wrapped his fingers around her hand.

Martin started explaining the events.

Andy excused himself and Shandra tried to release Ryan's hand.

He squeezed.

She peered into his eyes.

He shook his head slightly. She would ask Andy the same questions he had already asked.

Martin continued until the mosquitos became unbearable. "You'll see tomorrow what all it takes to prepare for a traditional feast."

"We'll see you then," Ryan helped Shandra to her feet and they walked back to the house hand in hand.

"You talked to Andy?" she asked.

"Yes." He relayed what he'd learned from her cousin. "He says Coop and Sandy will be here tomorrow night and they would be the best people to ask about Tripp, Pim, and Nelly. They are closer in age and would have been in school with them."

"Good idea." Shandra led him upstairs to the room they shared.

She pulled the letter from her grandmother out of her purse and tapped it against the palm of her other hand.

"Read it. I bet it's nothing more than telling you she knew you'd come back," Ryan kissed her cheek and grabbed his pajamas and shave kit. He'd take a shower while she read the letter.

Shandra watched Ryan walk out of the room. She didn't know why she was reluctant to read the letter. "Maybe because of the guilt I feel for not getting to know her before she died."

She picked up Ryan's pocket knife that was sitting on the bedside table with his phone and wallet, and sliced the envelope open.

Granddaughter,

When you were born and I held you, I could tell you would grow up to be beautiful and strong. You had to be strong. Your mother took you from us and you had to deal with life alone.

If you are reading this letter, you are no longer alone. You have come back to your family. Use that same strength to find peace with the past and embrace the gifts the Creator bestowed upon you.

My only regret is not fighting harder to keep you in our arms. But you are back, and I rest well.
I will see you in your dreams,
Ella

Happy tears spilled down her cheeks. Grandmother had known she'd find her way home.

~*~

Shandra stared out the kitchen window. Men, women, and children wore their best shirts and dresses adorned with ribbons. "Everyone looks so festive in their ribbon shirts and dresses." She'd noted both Aunt Jo and Velma had worn a ribbon dress. Velma's was covered with a thick cloth apron at the moment.

Velma grabbed at the wooden ten-inch-long skewers Shandra held in her hands. "It's a celebration, of course everyone would wear their ribbon clothing. Right now, it's our job to get this salmon ready to cook."

Shifting her attention back to the job, she watched as her aunt skillfully ran a four-foot-long one-and-a-half-inch in diameter stick up the full length of a salmon fillet from the head end to within four inches of the tail end.

"You have to keep this in the widest part of the meat along the spine and not stick it through the skin." Velma had told her the sticks were made of ironwood and had been passed down through her family to be used for cooking salmon.

"Where did all these salmon come from?" Shandra asked. She'd been in awe when a young man had arrived early this morning with two large coolers in the back of his pickup. All the salmon he'd arrived with were now filleted and waiting to be skewered on the ironwood sticks.

"I asked the men of the family to catch them for this celebration." Velma held the first fillet she'd worked the stick into. "This is what you will do. Watch carefully. When I get a stick in one like this. You are going to use these small pieces in your hand, like this, to keep the fish on the stick." Her aunt pushed the smaller sticks through the fillet from side to side, further attaching the fish to the larger stick. "Then stack them in that cooler. The boys will come get them when the fire is ready."

As the two of them worked on the salmon, women came and went in the kitchen, putting foods they brought together or gathering items that would be needed for the feast.

It took Shandra half a dozen fish before she finally inserted the skewers without the fillet looking like a porcupine on a bad hair day. When she didn't have to concentrate as hard, she decided to question her aunt.

"Wendy and Tripp make a nice couple," she said, by way of starting the conversation.

Velma stopped shoving the stick in the fillet and stared at her for several seconds, then went back to work. "Wendy could find better. I'm hoping while she's teaching in Spokane she will find a nice man."

"She could find one there who will take her away from the reservation and her traditions," Shandra hedged.

Velma slapped a fillet on the large wooden board she'd brought with her. "She would never fall for a man who does not believe in our traditions."

"Sometimes love is blind. You get sucked into the thought someone could love you for who you are and then realize too late they are changing you." She didn't like to talk about herself, but she was the poster child for starting her romantic life off in a bad relationship.

"She's too strong for that to happen." Velma shoved a stick into the fillet with more force.

"Do you think I'm strong?" She hadn't told her aunt what had happened to her but from past conversations, Velma knew. Her sight had told her when Shandra had been at her worst.

"You are, and you got out." Velma didn't look at her, but her motions were less violent.

"I was lucky someone helped me find my strength. Tripp seems to love Wendy and doesn't have a problem with her teaching the traditions at the college. How could you not like their relationship?" She was siding with the two young people to get her aunt's reactions. Deep down she wondered at the odd couple.

Velma handed her another skewered fillet and grabbed one out of the cooler. "He has changed. Others of the Seven Drums have noticed it. He's calmer, less prone to angry outbursts. His drumming has been healing for his soul. But his past… I don't want my daughter hurt by his poor choices in high school and beyond."

"I understand. But maybe he deserves this second chance?" She glanced out the window and spotted Ryan visiting with Logan. The big tribal policeman word a red shirt with blue and yellow ribbons. "Will Mrs. Rider be here today?"

"She was invited. If Logan isn't working, I'm sure he will bring her." Velma had six fillets piled up for Shandra to put her skewers through. "Hurry. These are the last of them."

"Is this enough for all the people?" She didn't think they had enough salmon to fill everyone.

"Jo is also making a large pot of deer stew. No one will leave here hungry." Velma picked up one of the fillets. She had two finished with the cross skewers by the time Shandra finished one. "The more you do this the faster you will become."

Shandra glanced at her aunt. "I know this is a tradition, but I doubt I'll be cooking a salmon on an open fire any time soon on Huckleberry Mountain."

Velma smiled. "You will have many celebrations to help with the salmon. You are young."

She had an odd sensation her aunt had dreamed something.

Velma hurried out the door as Shandra washed her hands.

Two young men entered. Each one grabbed an end to the cooler with the prepared fish, picked up the cooler, and walked out the door.

Curious about what was happening outside, Shandra tucked her phone in her back pocket, grabbed her sunglasses, and plopped her cowgirl hat on her head. One step outside the house and she found herself pulled into the tide of people walking to the field a half a mile away.

Two teepees stood in the middle of the field. Smoke rose from a fire burning between the two structures. Makeshift tables of hay bales and lumber stretched out in a line. There were already bowls and platters of food on the tables along with stacks of paper plates and plastic utensils. She smiled at the use of modern conveniences at a traditional celebration feast.

Jo stood by the fire stirring what Shandra figured

must be the deer stew in a large cast iron kettle.

Children played games of hide and seek and a stick game she remembered Grandmother teaching her the summer she'd run away to the reservation.

Teens and young adults were gathered in groups talking and looking at their cell phones. The older people sat on bales of hay, visiting.

She finally found Ryan, Andy, and Coop. All three walked up to the fire and dumped armloads of wood next to the pit. Old Moses was tending the fire.

Before she could make her way to the three men, a pickup pulled up with Velma in the back and the cooler of fish. Andy and Coop lifted the cooler down and Velma's husband stepped out of the front of the pickup and helped Velma down. She nodded to her husband and followed the cooler to the fire. Her aunt had taken off the apron. Her sky blue dress with pink, purple and orange ribbons was festive.

After Coop and Andy raised the lid, Velma stepped forward and grasped the salmon on top. She walked over to the fire and set the stick into a metal frame that ran the perimeter of the fire. She placed six fillets on all four sides of the fire and picked up a long stick that she used to move the logs on fire closer to the edge. When the middle of the fire was cleared, she gently tossed more wood into the center.

Aunt Jo walked up beside Shandra.

"How long does it take the fish to cook?" Shandra asked.

"About an hour."

"She only put half of the fish out there." Her stomach was already growling.

"We will start eating when the first batch is done

and continue to eat until it is all gone." Aunt Jo moved back to the large kettle and stirred the contents.

Shandra scanned the immediate area for Ryan. She caught a glimpse of Wendy and Tripp disappearing through some of the parked cars.

Chapter Fifteen

Ryan had found everything about this day interesting. From the apple and alder wood he and the Elwood boys had cut up for the fire, to the way everyone had known their jobs and set about doing it without being directed.

He'd planned to join Shandra after delivering the last load of wood but the placing of the salmon around the fire had drawn his attention. Then Coop grabbed him and they headed to one of the teepees.

"What are we doing in here?" Ryan asked. Several old trunks with what looked like buckskins and feathers flowing out of them stood along one side. Flamboyant headdresses and staffs hung from leather thongs on the tent poles.

"Finding you something to dance in tonight." Coop smiled at him and headed for one of the trunks.

"I'm not sure others would like that," he said.

"You're marrying Shandra. That makes you family. You'll dance with the rest of us."

"Why do we need clothes? All of your family are wearing clothes that seem right for dancing." Ryan had noticed the colorful shirts and dresses on Shandra's family members and others who had come to the event.

"This is a ribbon shirt. It is our contemporary way of dressing traditionally." Coop pulled out what looked to be a breechcloth.

"I'm not wearing that. I'll find a ribbon shirt." Ryan pointed to the tanned leather.

Coop laughed. "I should dress you in this. Then the others would laugh, but I'll be nice. Ays?"

"Why are you digging out the clothing now? The dancing won't happen until after we eat."

"If we don't pick out your clothing now, you may end up in only a breechcloth." Coop handed him the two garments. "Take these to my pickup until it's time to change. It's closer than yours."

Ryan nodded and ducked out of the tepee, heading toward Coop's pickup parked over where they'd cut the wood. He glanced to his right in time to see Shandra wandering through the parked cars behind the food tables.

He changed course. Who was she following and why? With the bundle of clothes under his arm, he kept an eye on Shandra's cowgirl hat as she ducked between vehicles.

He lost sight of her and rounded a pickup. Her hat came into view seconds before he tripped over her. Shandra crouched at the bumper of the pickup.

"What are you doing?" he asked in a low tone.

She jumped and spun, looking up at him. "I'm following Tripp and Wendy. Get down."

He knelt behind her. "Why?"

"Because they snuck away." Her tone insinuated it made perfect sense.

"You are becoming a stalker," he said light-heartedly.

She shook her head. "I'm protecting my cousin."

"We don't know who killed Nelly and I doubt whoever did would kill Wendy. The only thing they have in common is Tripp."

"The reservation playboy." Shandra pivoted back around. "They're gone." She stood.

Ryan stood and grasped her hand. "The people we need to talk to are Coop and Sandy. I have to put these clothes in Coop's truck. Maybe we'll find them in the process."

Shandra put a hand on the breastplate. "What are these for?"

"According to your cousin, I'm dancing tonight and have to wear the costume." He liked the way her eyes lit up at the notion.

"Really? We're both dancing?" She hugged his arm. "I can't wait."

They put the clothing in Coop's pickup and returned to the feasting area. Coop stood beside the tables laden with food. Ryan thought it would be a good time to get Coop and Sandy off somewhere to talk before things became too crazy. He led Shandra over to her cousin.

"I wish those fish would finish cooking," Coop said, picking up a handful of potato chips and staring at the cooking salmon.

Shandra grabbed a handful of chips as her stomach grumbled. "I agree."

The smell of the cooking fish made Ryan's

stomach remember it had been a long time since breakfast. He grabbed a bag of chips and nodded. "We'd like to visit with you and Sandy."

Coop scanned the area. "She's over there. Talking to Ruby. I'll get her."

Ryan held the chip bag out to Shandra as Coop's long legs covered the space between them and Sandy quickly.

"Where are we going to talk?" Shandra asked, grabbing a handful of the chips. "It's getting too hot to stand out here in the sun."

Coop returned with Sandy's hand clasped in his. "How about we walk down by the creek."

"Sounds good to us," Ryan said, offering the bag of chips to the couple.

They each took some and led the way toward the line of trees about seventy-five yards from the feast.

Ryan moved up beside the two. "How well did you both know Nelly Bingham?"

Coop didn't look at him, but Sandy's head swiveled on her neck.

"You want to talk to us about Nelly?" she asked.

"Not just Nelly but Pim Solomon and Tripp Talman," Ryan held the bag out again.

"You pretty much know all there is to know about Nelly. She used her body to get boys and men to start using for Duke Waters." Coop shrugged. "She was someone you pitied but stayed away from because of the rumors or lies that would be spread."

"What do you mean by that?" Shandra asked as they entered the shade of the trees.

"If a guy so much as came within a hundred yards of Nelly, if she thought you could be coerced into using or selling drugs, she'd start rumors you and her were an item to get you to do what she wanted." Coop scowled. "She tried that on a couple of my friends. But we managed to beat the rumors down."

Shandra stopped and stared at her cousin. "She was that manipulative to help Duke Waters?"

Sandy nodded. "If you were a girl, she'd spread rumors about you that would get you in trouble with parents or the school or a boyfriend if you had one. She would stoop to anything to get a person selling or using."

"I don't know what Duke gave her when she pulled someone in, but she worked her ass off for him." Coop sat down cross-legged in a grassy spot by the stream.

Shandra and Ryan sat across from him. Sandy sat in the circle of Coop's legs.

"We heard that Nelly stole Tripp from Pim when you were all in high school. What do you know about that?" Ryan asked, taking a handful of chips and placing the bag in between them.

Sandy looked up over her shoulder at Coop. He shrugged. "Kind of the usual. Pim didn't put out and Tripp found someone who did."

Shandra shook her head not liking the way Tripp came across and knowing he was sweet-talking her innocent cousin somewhere. "Was Tripp selling or using then?"

"I don't think so. I think Nelly went out with him to make Duke jealous." Coop grabbed the bag and offered it to Sandy.

"It wasn't long after that Nelly was pregnant," Sandy added.

"Nelly swore Duke was the father, but when he

requested a paternity test, she refused. Any thoughts on that?" Ryan asked.

"Rumors back then were that Tripp had offered to marry Nelly and she'd turned him down, saying the baby was Duke's and he would take care of them." Sandy put a chip in her mouth and crunched.

Shandra sat up straighter. "What do you two think? Is Tripp Fawn's father?"

Coop stared in her eyes. "I hope not. Mom is too attached to that little girl to have some bad influence like Duke or Tripp take her away."

She had the same thoughts and feelings. But if Tripp was the father, had he been putting the money in the mailbox all these years? "What does Tripp do for work?"

"He works construction around the reservation and at The Dam," Coop said.

"Has he had a job since school?" If he was the father, what would Nelly possibly have had over him that he didn't want coming out? That he was the father? Was he afraid Wendy would reject him if she knew the truth?

"Yeah, he's always had a knack for finding work," Coop said.

"His only flaw is not being able to stick with a girl once he conquers her," Sandy said.

"What do you mean by that?" Shandra had a notion she knew but wanted to be sure.

Coop's face flushed. "He's known to pick good girls and get them to fall for him. Then he takes them to bed and the next thing you know he has moved on to another one."

Shandra stared at him. "And Wendy?"

"So far she's kept him in line and kept her dignity," Sandy said.

"But you think once he talks her into taking their relationship further, he'll move on?" Shandra didn't like Tripp as much as before.

"The only way he'll stay is if she gets him to marry her before that happens." Coop played with Sandy's hair. "And I think he's wily enough to not fall for that, because one thing about Tripp, if he is with a girl, he's loyal until he moves on. If he were bound to her by marriage, he'd be obligated to stay."

Shandra found the young man's ideals conflicting. He was loyal, but once he got what he wanted or won the prize, she guessed in his eyes, he ended the relationship and moved on to a new conquest or game. "Do you think that's what Wendy has in mind? Getting Tripp to marry her first?"

Coop shrugged. "Who knows. She's Velma's daughter and that woman has strange ideas."

Ryan laughed. "That I can agree with."

Shandra nudged her shoulder against Ryan's. "That's my family you're talking about."

He sobered. "I know. What more can you tell us about Duke Waters back then and now? Especially, how did he treat people who wanted out of the business?"

Coop glanced down at Sandy. She fidgeted with her hands in her lap. "We're not sure, but we think Nelly might be the one who got Butch started selling drugs." Coop wrapped an arm around Sandy. "Back then it didn't take much to get Butch into anything. He was always looking for a thrill."

Shandra could see it was hard for Sandy to think

about her brother as a drug dealer. But it had been Sandy who had helped the FBI crackdown on the drugs coming into the reservation. It was her finding and turning over Butch's ledger that slowed the drug trade for a while and put her brother in jail.

"Do you think Butch would have any information on who he thinks would have wanted to hurt Nelly?" Shandra asked.

Sandy shook her head. Staring Shandra in the eyes she said, "Butch is pretty mad at me. I don't think he'd talk to anybody who knows me."

Coop wrapped his arms around Sandy. "It's not your fault he got into drugs. He was old enough and smart enough to know better. You did the best you could." He glanced up at Ryan and Shandra. "Are you thinking Duke had something to do with Nelly's death?"

Ryan gave a dismissive shrug and glanced at Shandra. She studied Ryan. Would he tell these two all he knew?

As if he read her thoughts, Ryan studied Coop and Sandy and grabbed the potato chip bag. "At this point we're not sure who could have killed her. I've been kept out of the loop because I'm not part of the tribal police or an FBI agent. We had a little talk with Duke. I don't believe anything he said. However, unless he can be placed at the agency or near the Community Center at the time of Nelly's death, we don't have anything on him. We do know he was mad because she had told him she wanted out and was headed to school in Spokane."

Coop nodded his head. "Duke didn't like anyone quitting on him. The only reason Billy Crow got out of selling was because he became a drunk. Duke couldn't rely on him to bring back the correct amount of money for the drugs he sold."

Sandy straightened. "I've wondered if Duke had anything to do with Wesley Tibble's death."

"Wesley Tibble?" Ryan asked, handing the potato chip bag to Shandra.

Sandy looked over her shoulder at Coop. "Remember how we were all trying to figure out how Wesley could have drowned in the lake when he was an excellent swimmer?"

"Yeah, we heard that he had worked for Duke. And he'd wanted to marry Pim Solomon, but she wouldn't marry him as long as he sold drugs." Coop's eyes widened, and his mouth dropped open. "Do you think she had something to do with Nelly's death?"

Shandra was having the same thought as her cousin. Pim seemed to have a lot of pent-up anger in her. And she could see the young woman taking revenge. She was bright enough that she would've tried to pin it on someone else.

"This does make me wonder about Pim," Ryan said. He glanced at Shandra. "Do you know if Pim was invited to the party?"

"I don't know who was invited." Shandra peered across the open space between them and her cousin. "Do you have any idea?"

"The only person who can answer that question would be Velma," Coop said.

Ryan stood and held out his hand to Shandra. "Don't talk to anybody about what we said. We don't need another death on this reservation."

Shandra stood and nodded. "I'm looking forward

to the dinner and the dancing tonight." She glanced between Coop and Sandy. "Are you two dancing?"

Sandy's cheeks reddened, and she nodded. "We are. Velma picked us to show you the courting dance."

Shandra smiled down at the pair. "I'm so glad it will be you two." She looked over her shoulder at Ryan and smiled. "This is going to be the best night of my life."

Ryan led her away from the other couple and said under his breath, "I hope it is."

Chapter Sixteen

Shandra couldn't believe how much she'd eaten. Between the delicious fish, the savory deer stew, potato, macaroni, and taco salads, and delicious fry bread that were provided by everyone, she felt as if her stomach would explode. She hadn't even ventured toward the dessert table covered with pies and cakes.

Now she was in the women's teepee with several other young women who were going to dance, putting on a traditional dress.

"Shandra that looks wonderful on you," Sandy said, standing near the door in a traditional dress and knee-high moccasins.

Wendy handed Shandra a comb. "Comb your hair into two braids. We'll tie this feather into some strands. It means you are unmarried."

"If all goes well that will be taken care of in a few more weeks," Shandra said, feeling giddy about participating in the dancing and the notion she and Ryan would soon be married.

Wendy's cheeks grew redder, and her eyelashes fluttered down to rest on her cheeks. "Yes, but you are unmarried by white society. Since you and Ryan have been living together, the Indian ceremony, is only a formality. You are already husband and wife by the old ways."

She hadn't meant to cause her cousin any embarrassment. But in this day and age she had to believe that Wendy knew as much about the physical aspects of a man and a woman as anyone else her age. Velma couldn't have kept her that much in the dark. Especially, considering who she was dating.

Wendy stepped away from Shandra to another area of the teepee to dress in her own regalia.

Sandy moved over next to Shandra. "Coop talked to Velma. Pim was invited and is here," she whispered.

Shandra nodded her head and thought about this new information. She had a hard time believing that the young woman could have shoved a knife into Nelly hard enough to cause the damage Ryan told her about. But at the same time, she understood how badly Pim and her mother wanted the scholarship. With all the medical expenses for Mrs. Solomon, whatever grants they received from the government wasn't going to cover all the costs of Pim living in Spokane and attending classes. Shandra wondered if it was Pim's desire for the scholarship or if she'd finally mustered the courage to deal revenge for Wesley Tibble's death.

But if she was out for revenge, she would have placed evidence to make it appear as if Duke killed Nelly. So far, Ryan said there was very little evidence other than the body.

The women filed out of the structure one by one.

Shandra would have taken up the rear if Wendy hadn't ushered her out ahead of her.

The golden glow of the setting sun, the raging fire, and the people gathered around, most in ribbons shirts and some in everyday clothes gave an ethereal feeling to the evening. Some men were already dancing. The singing and drums echoed around her as if she were in a 3-D movie theater. The images were shadowed with golden halos.

Velma arrived at her side. "Come."

She followed her aunt to a spot where Aunt Jo, Uncle Martin, Andy, and Fawn sat on bales. Her aunt patted the bale next to her.

She sat and leaned toward her aunt. "Have you seen Ryan?"

Jo pointed to a line of men in regalia. It wasn't hard to pick him out of the group. He was the only one taking in everything. The others seemed to be drawing into themselves, their feet stepping to the music even though they remained in line. The drumming stopped.

"All those joining in the celebration dance form your circles," an elder called out.

Jo urged Shandra to stand. "Do what the other women do."

Shandra walked out to the circle the women were forming.

A bell tinkled and the drumming began. The other women did small side steps to the beat of the drums. She followed and her mind absorbed the beats and the voices wailing in song. Her heart and feet moved to the pounding in her head. Shadows fell across her and the women on either side of her. She started and glanced up to see the men stomping and turning in a circle around the women. Her mind moved from the song, making her feet stumble as she watched each man go by.

Ryan was stomping and only turning side to side, not making a full circle when he danced past her.

She made note of how well the buckskin clung to his muscular legs. Knowing he was included in the dance, she allowed herself to dive back into the music. Slowly, she lost sense of the now and floated above the circles, tapping dancers on the head as if playing duck, duck, goose or counting coup.

The second the counting coup came to mind, she dropped back within herself. Counting coup meant they were the enemy and she was proving her strength or power by tapping them. These people weren't her enemy. Most were family. Shook by the experience and thoughts, she stumbled out of the line.

Ryan saw Shandra fumbling through the dancing men and went to her aid. "What's wrong?"

He grabbed her shoulders and gave her a gentle shake. "Shandra, what did you see?"

She shook her head.

He drew her away from the dancing, through the watching crowd, and into the dark cool air outside the spectators.

"It…I've never…" She stared at him as if she didn't know what to say.

"Did you see your grandmother?" he asked.

"No. I floated above everyone and tapped them on the head, like…like counting coup." She shuddered.

Ryan studied the level-headed woman he loved. "You tapped everyone? Dancers and those watching?"

She shook her head. "Just dancers." She closed her eyes. "Not all of them. I didn't tap you." Her eyes opened. "I touched Wendy, Pim, and Tripp."

He narrowed his eyes. "Tripp isn't dancing. He's pounding on the drum."

"It was his face I saw when I tapped him." She thought a minute. "And Duke." Her head swiveled. "Is he here?"

"I don't think you were counting coup. I think your grandmother was making sure you knew all the players in the murder were here." Ryan grasped her hand, leading her back to the dancing and the bales where her immediate family sat. Fawn had fallen asleep on Martin's lap.

"Why did you leave the dance?" Jo asked, worry creasing her brow.

Shandra glanced at Ryan. "I don't know. A feeling came over me. I just felt like I needed some air."

Martin nodded. "It's hot, they make it hotter with that fire, and I bet you haven't had enough water today."

Ryan released her hand. "I bet that's it. I'll go grab a couple bottles of water."

Shandra grabbed his arm. "Be careful," she whispered.

He nodded and worked his way through the crowd to the coolers icing the cans of soda and bottles of water. As he bent to grasp two bottles of water, he heard a familiar voice.

Duke.

Shandra's vision had been correct. He was here. Why? This was a private property.

Keeping his back to the voice, Ryan worked his way through the people mingling around the drinks. When Ryan judged he was behind Duke, he turned and ran into the back of Officer Logan Rider.

The big man put an arm around Ryan's shoulders. "Look who slithered in."

"That's what I was trying to do when you blocked my view."

Logan laughed and took one of the bottles of water from him. "Good one. We'll make an Indian out of you yet. *Ays*?"

Ryan had learned when they made a joke, the people of the reservation added the *ays* to the end of the sentence. Most of the time he thought the added word was funnier than the joke. This was one of those times.

"Why do you think Duke came here?" Ryan opened his bottle and drank, making a mental note that he needed to grab another one for Shandra when he finished his conversation with Logan.

"From who he has talked to so far, he is fishing for information." Logan frowned.

"Information? Is he asking about Fawn or Nelly?" Ryan hoped the man didn't cause a scene over the child. And it struck him. Logan had been watching the man since he arrived. He was a good cop.

"He is trying to discover what we," he narrowed his eyes, "the Tribal Police, have and who the FBI agent in charge is."

"You think he's greasing FBI hands to get his drugs in here?" Ryan took another swallow of his drink and didn't try to hide when Duke looked his way. The drug dealer frowned at Logan watching him and moved through the crowd.

"I better get back to Shandra. She had a…" he wasn't sure what to call it. "She about passed out from the heat."

Logan put a hand on his shoulder. "Is she okay? My grandmother said she is special. Carries her grandmother's magic. We must keep her safe."

"She had an experience while dancing that upset her." He nodded the direction Duke had disappeared. "She'd known he was here."

Logan nodded and raised his hand. "I'll keep track of him. You go tend to Shandra."

"I will." Ryan hurried back by the drinks, grabbed another bottle of water, and found Shandra standing by her family.

He handed the bottle to her and said in a low voice. "He's here. Logan has been watching him."

She studied him. "How did he get here?"

"Ask your aunt."

"Jo or Velma?" She took a drink of water.

"Both." He shrugged.

Shandra faced Jo and motioned for her to join them.

Her aunt stood and walked over, a puzzled expression wrinkling her brow. "Yes?"

"Why would Duke Waters be here?" Shandra asked.

Her aunt visibly shuddered. "Why indeed!"

"Don't cause a scene," Ryan said. "He's here and we would like to know why he would be allowed at a family event."

Jo stared at him as if he'd just sprouted floppy ears and whiskers. "Everyone is family during a celebration ceremony. But we would not have invited a known drug dealer." She pivoted toward her husband.

Ryan put a hand on her arm to stop her.

She spun back around toward him.

"Don't say anything. Logan is keeping an eye on him. We want to see who he talks to. I just wondered at why he would have come to an Elwood-Higheagle ceremony." He smiled, hoping to ease her frustration.

"I don't want him causing trouble for Fawn," the woman said in a low tone.

"I don't think he will. If he hasn't claimed her by now, he has no intention of ever doing it," Shandra said, putting an arm around her aunt's shoulders.

"I hope so. She's a darling."

It was apparent Shandra's aunt had become attached to the child already.

The drumming and singing stopped. The dancers moved into a large circle.

Velma stepped into the circle. "Coop Elwood and Sandy Baxter have agreed to show our soon-to-be-wed Shandra Higheagle and Ryan Greer the courting dance."

Ryan clasped a hand with one of Shandra's and they walked to the edge of the dancers to watch Coop and Sandy. If he hadn't known better he would have thought they'd stepped back in time, watching the dancers in costume making the circle around the couple dressed in traditional buckskins.

Coop stood in the middle of the circle with a blanket pulled around him. The drums beat slow and low. Sandy tapped her feet on the ground and spun in circles around Coop, waving a bright shawl wrapped around her shoulders. When he opened his blanket, she danced away. They did this several times. Then Sandy slowed her dance. It resembled a butterfly trying to find a place to land. This time when Coop opened the blanket she entered, the drum boomed once loudly, and the crowd cheered.

Coop and Sandy walked over to them. "Now, it is your turn." Coop handed the blanket to Ryan.

"Just dance how you feel," Sandy said, placing the shawl around Shandra's shoulders.

Ryan studied Shandra. "Are you ready?"

She nodded and they walked out to the middle of the circle. He knew he had the easy job. All he had to do was open his blanket when Shandra came near him. He was curious if she would instinctively know what to do.

The drum started. She pranced around him twice before approaching slightly. He opened his blanket, she winked and pranced away. If he hadn't been standing in the middle of her whole family, he would have laughed and chased after her.

She danced toward him a second time.

A scream rang out in the cool night air.

Chapter Seventeen

Shandra froze, staring the direction the shriek had sounded. As one, the spectators moved that direction. Shandra followed with Ryan on her heels. When the crowd became too compacted, Ryan stepped in front of her, clearing a path.

She stopped cold as the four people she'd tapped in her dance trance appeared in front of her.

Logan had Duke by the arm. A bloody antler-handled knife lay on the ground between those two and Wendy and Tripp. Pim stood to the side, staring at Tripp. Her eyes were wide and filled with concern. She clearly still loved him. What kind of hold did this young man have over women? Nelly had wanted him to go to Spokane with her, Pim still loved him, and Wendy defied her mother to remain with him.

Wendy had her hand pressed to Tripp's side. Blood oozed through her fingers, dripping onto her buckskin dress and Tripp's jeans.

"Call nine-one-one," Ryan said, standing over the knife.

Shandra moved to Wendy's side. "He can't be too hurt, he's still standing."

Tripp gave her a half smile, but his color was draining.

"Get Tripp something to sit on!" Ryan shouted.

Shandra eased him onto the bale of hay that Coop brought over. Wendy sank to his side, her hand still on the bleeding wound.

Logan put Duke's arms behind his back and pulled a pair of handcuffs out of his pocket.

"Were you expecting trouble?" Ryan asked.

Logan grinned. "When there is celebrating, someone always gets out of control." He glanced around and motioned to two men. "Take him about thirty yards over there and don't let him get away."

The two nodded.

"I didn't do anything. This is police harassment!" Duke hollered as the two dragged him away from the rest of the people involved.

Shandra didn't move when Logan crouched in front of Tripp. "You okay to answer a few questions?"

The younger man nodded.

"Did you see who knifed you?" Logan asked, nodding to the bloody weapon on the ground at Ryan's feet.

Glancing from the knife to Ryan's face, she noticed he was keeping an eye on Pim, who had two men standing on either side of her. She wondered when Logan had given the order for that to happen. Shandra shifted her attention back to Tripp.

He shook his head. "Didn't see anything. Wendy and I were talking at the edge of the crowd. I felt something shove into my side. I put a hand over it and spotted the knife on the ground. Wendy screamed, and everyone showed up." He closed his eyes and drew in a deep breath.

Logan studied Wendy. "Did you see anything?"

Her cousin's gaze flashed to Pim, then the direction Duke had been led and continued to shout, before returning to Logan. "My back was to whoever did it. I can't be certain."

Logan stood and did a slow spin. "Anyone here see anything that will help us find out who stabbed young Tripp?"

Pim stepped forward. "It was Duke. I saw him with the knife earlier."

Shandra felt Wendy snap her head around and peer at the young woman. When her cousin noticed she'd caught Shandra's attention, she dropped her gaze to where her hand rested on Tripp.

Something was off. Shandra felt the tension between Wendy and Pim. The animosity practically crackled in the air, yet, Wendy kept quiet about something she knew about Pim.

"Why would Duke want to knife Tripp?" Logan asked Pim.

She shrugged.

Andy ran up to Logan, holding out a pack that looked a lot like Ryan's forensic pack.

"Thanks." Logan pulled out two pairs of latex gloves. He handed a set to Ryan and tugged a set on his hands.

When Ryan had his gloves on, he picked up the

knife, studied it without touching any area that might have picked up prints, and settled it into the paper bag Logan opened toward him.

Shandra could tell, Ryan had found something interesting about the knife.

Andy and Coop now stood behind her. Shandra turned to Andy. "Is there an ambulance coming?"

He nodded. "But it would be quicker to load him into a truck and haul him to the county road."

She had wondered about that. With all the cars parked everywhere, there wasn't a clear path for an ambulance to get close. "Logan, should Andy and Coop take Tripp down to the county road so the ambulance can pick him up?"

The policeman glanced her direction. "When I've finished questioning them."

She nodded, realizing it was the first time the man had used an authoritative tone with her. Had she overstepped her concern for Tripp or did he feel she was butting into his investigation? She glanced at Ryan, but he was conferring with Logan.

The large Tribal Policeman nodded and headed over to Duke with Ryan on his heels.

Shandra shifted her attention to Tripp and her cousin. "Why wasn't Tripp drumming?"

"The song only needed one drummer." Wendy peered into Tripp's eyes.

He nodded. "We walked over here where it was quieter just to talk." He glanced over Wendy's shoulder toward Pim who stared at the two.

The other young woman had steeled her expression. The love Shandra had witnessed earlier no longer burned in her eyes. Had Pim knifed a young man she loved to put blame on the drug dealer who killed her first love? A headache was coming on. It could be from the heat, the daydream as she danced, the tangled web these people were all a part of, or all of it.

Velma arrived. "Wendy, get up from there." She grabbed her daughter's arm.

"Velma, no. She's stopping the bleeding," Shandra said, easing Velma away from the two.

Her aunt glared at Tripp. "This is what I feared when Wendy started dating you."

"Tripp didn't ask to be knifed," Shandra said, drawing her aunt's attention from the two young people.

"Maybe not, but trouble follows him. A cloud shrouds his life. I don't want that for my daughter." Velma glared at Shandra. "Why do you stick up for him? He could have killed Nelly."

"If that's what Logan finds, then we'll treat him accordingly, but for now he is innocent." Shandra led Velma further away from the people involved in the stabbing. "What can you tell me about Pim and Tripp's past?"

Velma studied her. "Why? Do you think they are in this together?" The woman's gaze drifted back and forth between the two Shandra had mentioned.

"It was a look Pim gave him. As if she still loved him."

Velma snorted. "She could do better than the likes of him. Just like my Wendy."

"When were they together? Before or after Wesley Tibble died?" Shandra asked.

Her aunt stared at her. "Wesley Tibble? He died in an accident about three years ago. Why would you want to know about him?"

"Was that before or after Pim says Nelly took Tripp away from her?" Shandra wanted to get the timeline straight in her head. This small group of young people switched partners as much as characters on a soap opera.

"It would have been after Tripp dumped her for Nelly." Velma studied her closely. "You think Pim killed Nelly out of jealousy and tried to kill Tripp?" Her face froze in horror seconds before her eyes became glowing orbs of anger. "Wendy is in danger if she stays with Tripp." The woman took one step and Shandra grabbed her arm.

"I don't think Wendy is in danger. She and Pim appear to have animosity but they also seem together in something." Shandra studied the two. Wendy still sat beside Tripp. Pim stood with her arms crossed, glaring at Ryan and Logan questioning Duke.

~*~

"Why did you come here tonight?" Ryan asked the drug dealer. He wished it was his collar, then he could take the man in for questioning. But this wasn't his jurisdiction. Logan was being nice allowing him to ask questions.

"I was invited." Duke had feverishly stated he'd never seen that knife before in his life when Logan asked him about it.

"By who?" Ryan found it hard to believe anyone in Shandra's immediate family would have invited the man.

Duke sneered. "Andy Elwood."

Ryan shook his head. "I know better than that. Try again." While he was pretty sure Andy didn't have anything to do with drugs and wouldn't have invited this man, he was a cop and suspicious of everyone.

"Don't believe me? Ask him." Duke stood as insolent as he could with his wrists handcuffed behind him.

Ryan glanced at Logan.

"I'll print him and swab for blood residue while you ask Andy," the big policeman said.

Reluctant to get Shandra upset, Ryan wandered over to where Coop, Sandy, and Andy stood. Pretty sure the drug dealer was lying, Ryan faced Andy. "Did you invite Duke here?"

The young man's face drained of color. His gaze flicked to his older brother.

"Are you working for that scum?" Coop stepped toward Andy.

"No! I invited him because I knew Ryan and Shandra were interested in him for killing Nelly. She doesn't have many people who even care she died, but I wanted to make sure her killer is caught." Andy shoved his chest toward his brother as if he expected a fight.

"Chill. I know you and Nelly were friends." Coop faced Ryan. "I believe Andy thought he was helping you find Nelly's killer."

Ryan shook his head and addressed Andy. "Did you tell anyone you'd invited Duke here?"

He shook his head. "I was surprised that he actually came."

Velma's voice rose. Ryan saw anger on the woman's face and Shandra holding her back. He wondered what they were talking about, but knew he needed to relay what he'd just learned to Logan.

The big officer was talking to Pim. Ryan strolled

up as Logan asked, "Why did you come tonight?"

Pim shot a glance toward Wendy and Tripp before dropping her gaze to her feet. "Everyone is welcome at a celebration dance."

"This is true. But why did you come? I don't believe it was to dance in celebration." He tipped his head. "Or was it?"

Her chin came up, and she glared into his face. "What would I be celebrating?"

"Perhaps killing someone you were jealous of?" Logan said in a soft voice.

Ryan had different tactics for questioning, but the big man's soft easy manner seemed to work.

"I'll admit, I didn't like Nelly. Not many women on this reservation did. Have I wished her dead a thousand times? Yes." She continued to look Logan in the eyes.

Ryan moved up beside the officer. "Because she took Tripp from you or because she cost Wesley his life?"

Her whole body jerked, and she stared at him. "What do you know about Wesley?"

"Enough to know that you could have been harboring resentment and working your way up into getting revenge." Ryan didn't miss the flicker of anger in her eyes. His money was on this woman as the murderer and attempted murderer. The depth of her rage could very well propel her to pick up a knife and use it.

"Revenge won't bring Wesley back," she said and turned her attention to Logan. "May I go? I didn't see anything. I had come back here to get a breath of fresh air when Wendy screamed."

Logan let out a long, sigh. "You may go."

Ryan knew they had nothing at this time to hold her. He nodded his head toward Duke. "You taking him in for more questioning?"

"That depends. Did he get an invitation from Andy?" Logan glanced over Ryan's shoulder to where the brothers and Sandy stood.

Ryan hated to admit it. "Yeah. He knew Shandra and I had gone to the casino to talk to Duke and thought if he invited him here, we'd be able to see if he was acting suspicious."

Logan shook his head. "Now I have to let him go. He wasn't crashing so he had a legitimate reason to be here."

"Did you ever discover where he was when Nelly was stabbed?" Ryan asked. If Duke didn't have an alibi, he could be held on suspicion.

"I checked in on that and the employees at the casino. The security guard and his body guard both swear Duke was in the casino at the time of the murder. And both have previous records which makes me leery of their statements, but I haven't found anything to the contrary." Logan frowned.

"I was afraid of that," Ryan said.

Logan walked over to Duke and took the handcuffs off. "You may have been invited, but I'm asking you to leave. Now."

Duke shot a shit-eating grin at Ryan and disappeared through the crowd.

"Let's talk to the lovebirds again," Logan said, walking by Ryan toward Wendy and Tripp.

Ryan guessed the other man had noticed the little tells on both of them when they'd answered his first questions. The only problem was Velma stood behind her daughter, glaring at both of them.

"Velma, would you please step away while we ask these two a couple more questions?" Logan said it as if giving the woman a chance, but he took her by the arm and escorted her over to the Elwood boys, Sandy, and Shandra.

When Logan returned, he knelt on one knee in front of the two. "Can either of you give me a name of who would want to hurt Tripp?"

"When will an ambulance get here?" Wendy asked.

"I'm sure it is sitting at the end of the lane waiting for us to bring Tripp out." Logan put a hand on Wendy's shoulder.

"Tripp can you think of anyone lately that you've been in a quarrel with?"

The young man glanced at Wendy and said, "Nelly, but she's dead."

"No one else?" Logan probed.

Tripp shook his head.

"Wendy, can you think of anyone?" Logan removed his hand from her shoulder.

Ryan noticed she scanned the area, saw her mother was out of hearing, and said, "No one that Tripp has quarreled with, but Pim was glaring at me all night and she told me once if she couldn't have Tripp no one else could."

"Why didn't you say this before?" Ryan asked.

"I didn't want her to hear me. She might get madder." Wendy leaned her head on Tripp's shoulder.

Ryan opened the bag with the knife in it. "Have you seen this before?"

Her eyes widened and she leaned back, gawking at

Tripp. "That's the knife I gave you for your birthday."

"It was in my truck," Tripp said. "Under the seat in a sheath I'd made for it." The confusion on his face couldn't have been faked. "I was stuck with my own knife?"

Logan jumped in. "Who knows about the knife and where you keep it?"

Tripp winced while drawing in a deep breath. "Anyone I've talked to." He glanced at Wendy. "I'm proud of her work and like to show it off."

"Anyone here at the celebration?" Logan asked.

"About a dozen different people." Tripp's eyelids started drooping.

"Andy, Coop, take Tripp out to the ambulance." Logan stood and motioned for Ryan to follow him. "What do you make of this?" he asked.

Ryan glanced at Tripp being helped to a pickup. Wendy walked behind them and Shandra held onto Velma. "There are people here who know more than they're saying. What did you see Duke doing before the stabbing?"

"He talked with people we've suspected dealt in drugs, flirted with a couple of the younger women, and moved through the crowd as if searching for someone."

"Did he ever go near the Elwoods and Fawn?" Ryan found it curious if the man was the father, that he didn't have any interest in the child. Someone had been making that payment once a month to the Binghams.

"He didn't go near them. It wasn't as if he avoided them, but he clearly didn't go that direction." Logan nodded to Shandra and Velma. "You better go save Shandra."

"Let me know if you learn anything else." Ryan

walked over to the two women. He could see that Shandra was having a hard time with Velma.

"Does this mean the celebrating is over?" he asked the older woman.

"It is. I hope this isn't a sign about your wedding." Velma stormed off in the direction her daughter had gone.

Chapter Eighteen

Shandra hooked her arm in Ryan's. "Let's get out of these clothes and see if we can help with the clean-up." The crowd had started to disperse as Ryan and Logan talked with the people involved in the stabbing. All that remained were close family and a few friends who had begun cleaning up.

"Did you learn anything?" she asked as they walked toward the two teepees.

"Not really." He told her everything that was said.

"There's something between Wendy and Pim," she said when they needed to go to their separate teepees.

"What did you pick up on? More than Wendy being scared of Pim?" Ryan asked, hanging onto her hand.

"They don't like one another, which is realistic, but there's something else. Wendy is fearful of Pim. She knows something."

He nodded. "I had the same feeling. We need another talk with your cousin."

Shandra released his hand. "Tomorrow we can catch up with her and Tripp."

In the teepee, she spotted Wendy's clothing. She'd followed Tripp still dressed in her regalia. Shandra undressed and pulled on her regular clothes, then picked up Wendy's belongings, and stepped out of the teepee.

Pim stood to the side of the structure. She hadn't worn traditional clothing or joined in any of the dancing.

"Are you helping with clean-up?" Shandra asked.

"I wanted to speak to you." The young woman's gaze dropped to the clothing in Shandra's arms.

"What about?" Shandra hoped Ryan was still in the teepee. She wasn't comfortable being alone with Pim.

"The scholarship. Have you made a new decision?" The hopefulness in the women's voice made Shandra wish she could tell her she had the scholarship.

"We haven't had time to make a new decision. I promise we'll have a person picked by Monday."

Ryan exited the men's teepee.

Pim's gaze shot to him. "Thank you." She spun around and walked away.

"What was that about?" Ryan asked, joining her.

"She was asking about the scholarship, but I think she was lurking around the teepee to get her hands on these." Shandra held out Wendy's clothing and small leather purse.

"I say we leave the clean-up to the people who know what they're doing and return Wendy's belongings to her." Ryan put a hand on her lower back, urging her away from the celebration area and toward the house.

"I don't like leaving Aunt Jo." She glanced over her shoulder and saw two dozen people loading the wood and bales into pickups and carrying the trunks that held the traditional clothing out of the teepees. "I guess they do have things under control."

At Ryan's pickup, he turned on the inside lights. "Go through her pockets and check her purse. If you think Pim wanted Wendy's belongings there has to be a reason."

Shandra put her hands into the jean pockets and only found a couple sticks of gum and a five-dollar bill. There were no pockets in the shirt. She opened the doeskin shoulder bag, it was evident Wendy had made, and found a folded piece of paper.

"Careful, only touch the corners," Ryan said.

She lifted it out by the corners and touching only the points, opened the paper.

I KNOW WHAT YOU DID. YOU WILL PAY.

Shandra glanced over at Ryan. "This sounds like whoever wrote this believes Wendy killed Nelly. Do you suppose that's why they stabbed Tripp? To make her feel a loss, too?"

Ryan reached over the seat into the back of his extended cab and pulled his forensic bag onto his lap. He opened a large plastic evidence bag and pulled on one latex glove. Grasping the note by a corner, he placed it in the evidence bag, sealed it, and wrote the time and date on the bag.

"We'll ask Wendy about this. If Pim was after it, then she is possibly the one who sent it and stabbed Tripp." Ryan put his bag in the back, turned off the inside lights, and started up the pickup.

"But she had love in her eyes when she looked at

Tripp. Do you think she wanted revenge so badly she'd hurt a person she loved?" Shandra didn't think they had the recipient correct. "Maybe Tripp received the note, showed it to Wendy, and she put it in her purse?"

"But why didn't either of them mention it?" Ryan headed the vehicle down the lane.

Shandra shrugged. "I could tell Wendy was scared of Pim and the two didn't like one another."

"Call Logan and ask him where they took Tripp. That will be where we find Wendy and can ask her about the note." Ryan turned onto the county road and picked up speed.

"Do I tell Logan about the note we found?" She'd been chastised before by Ryan for withholding evidence because she wanted to ask someone a question.

"Yes. Tell him we'll meet him there." Ryan kept his attention on the road. This time of night any number of wildlife could decide to cross.

Shandra turned her phone on and found Logan in her contacts. His phone went straight to voicemail. "Logan, this is Shandra. I have Wendy's belongings and would like to get them to her. Where can we find her and Tripp? Also, we found an interesting note in Wendy's purse." She hit the off button. There was no need to go into detail on the phone.

"I left him a message."

Ryan glanced over at her. "Who else would know where they are taking Tripp?"

"I'll call Coop. He delivered Tripp to the ambulance." She found Coop's number and waited for him to answer.

"What's up Shandra?" he asked.

"Where was the ambulance taking Tripp?"

"The Dam, Coulee Medical Center. Is that why you and Ryan disappeared? Liz was looking for you." He didn't sound annoyed, more interested.

"We have Wendy's clothes and thought she might like them. I'm sorry I missed Liz. Is she still there? Maybe she could meet us at the medical center?" She knew Coop was hoping for something juicier but that was all she could give him.

He laughed. "That's a good reason to get out of cleaning up. *Ays*. If I see Liz again, I'll let her know where you are."

"Thanks. Will you and Sandy be around tomorrow to visit?" She wanted to change the subject.

"We won't go back to Spokane until Sunday night."

"Great. I'd like to visit with you about something other than this mess."

"See you tomorrow." Coop hung up.

She laughed.

"Is he unhappy you didn't tell him more?" Ryan asked.

"Yeah. I'm sure he'll grill us tomorrow." Shandra sat back in the seat. "He said the Coulee Medical Center at Grand Coulee."

He swung onto the highway and headed south. "So, off the reservation?"

"Yes. Cross the river below the dam and there should be a sign on the highway that will take us straight to the building."

Within minutes they were driving by the Community Center, Tribal building, and Trading Post. Ryan continued on down the highway at a legal speed.

Shandra sent out a prayer to find the truth as they passed the area where the metal shapes of the women root diggers stood off the side of the highway. They crossed the Columbia River and continued down the highway to Grand Coulee.

The building appeared to be fairly new. They drove around the building until they spotted the emergency entrance. Ryan parked and they both walked up to the doors.

Shandra peered through the large glass windows as Ryan pressed the entrance buzzer. Wendy sat in a chair, her head bent. She looked as if she'd lost everything.

A nurse appeared at the door. She scanned them both. "What's your emergency?"

"We don't have one. I'm Wendy's cousin," Shandra pointed to her cousin sitting in the waiting area. "I have her clothes."

The nurse let them in. "Please remain in the waiting area."

Shandra went straight to Wendy.

"What are you doing here?" her cousin asked, glancing up at them.

"I found your clothes in the teepee and thought you might want to change," Shandra placed everything in her cousin's lap.

"Thanks." She glanced toward the door. "Did mother come with you?"

"No. Do you want me to call her?" Shandra sat in the chair next to Wendy. Ryan stood a short distance away.

Wendy shuddered. "No. She's already mad at me for liking Tripp. I'm sure I'll get a talking to soon enough about how bad he is for me."

"Have they said anything about his condition?" Shandra asked.

"The doctor said he was lucky. The blade only nicked a couple of organs. They will all heal in time." Wendy flipped up the flap on her purse and froze. She'd been about to reach in and changed her mind.

"We have the note," Ryan said, walking closer. Up till now, he'd stayed back, but seeing how the woman had remembered the note at the last minute and hadn't wanted them to see it, he was interested in her explanation.

Wendy's gaze shot to him. "What note?"

He grinned. Typical evasive maneuver. "The one that was in your purse. The one that said 'I know what you did. You'll pay.'"

She flinched and glanced at Shandra.

"I'm sorry. I picked up your clothes to bring them to you. When Pim was lurking by the teepee and appeared interested in your things, we looked."

"Pim! I should have known she was the one who put that note in my purse." Wendy shoved her belongings to the side of the chair and stood. She paced back and forth.

"What did you do that she thinks you should pay for?" Ryan asked. The woman was upset more from who sent the note than the note itself. "Does it have anything to do with Nelly?"

Wendy stopped and stared at him. "Nelly? You think she saw me kill Nelly?" Her gaze narrowed on Shandra. "Is that what you think?"

"No. But I could tell you and Pim don't like one another." Shandra patted the chair her cousin had been sitting in. "Is it because of Tripp?"

Wendy seemed to believe Shandra. She sat, folding her fingers around her purse. "I'm not sure. Tripp said Pim is clingy. That once she believes she loves someone, she can't let them go."

"I've noticed that the girls Tripp dates tend to hang on to him. Nelly, Pim, can you name any others?" Shandra asked.

Ryan shifted, wondering what she was getting at.

Wendy stared at her cousin.

"Haven't you noticed how he tends to have very loyal past relationships?" Shandra touched Wendy's hand as if to break her from a trance.

"Now that you mention it, every girl he's dated would take him back if he looked their way." Wendy's brow furrowed.

"Any idea what Pim thinks you did?" Ryan asked, not understanding what the two women were really talking about.

Wendy's cheeks reddened. "I think I know, but if my mother ever found out, I would be the next murder you investigated."

Ryan glanced at Shandra. She seemed to understand but he was lost, again. "What might cause your mother to kill you?"

Shandra glared at him. "It's a figure of speech. Velma would never kill her child. She," Shandra tipped her head toward Wendy, "and Tripp have had sex."

Wendy's face turned bright red.

Now he understood. That was making Velma's good girl, not so good. "I see. And you think Pim found out. But why the threat?"

Wendy shook her head. "I don't know. Maybe she plans to tell mother." She shot to her feet. "Oh no! If she does…"

"But what would that gain her?" Ryan didn't see why Wendy and Tripp having sex would make Pim threaten her unless she planned to break them up, which telling Velma would do. Then Pim could sweep in and be Tripp's girl again. But it just didn't play out right in his mind. And why kill Nelly? It seemed Tripp wasn't interested in her at all anymore.

"This love triangle isn't helping with Nelly's murder or the reason Tripp was stabbed." Ryan paced over to the window and back to the two women. "Pim was quick to finger Duke for stabbing Tripp. We'll know who had anything to do with it when forensics comes back with fingerprints or DNA on the knife."

"I can't believe someone took the knife I gave Tripp and stabbed him with it." Wendy's eyes filled with tears. "It's my fault he's here."

"It's not your fault. It's the fault of the person who did it," Shandra said, patting her cousin's shoulder.

A door banged open down the hall.

Chapter Nineteen

Logan strode down the hall toward them. Shandra stood, placing a hand on Ryan's arm. The stern expression on Logan's face said he wasn't happy about something.

He bypassed them and strode right up to Wendy. "When was the last time you saw the knife you gave Tripp?"

Wendy started from his aggressive tone and leaned back. "I'm not sure. He showed it to some guys last week outside of the Ketch Pen."

"What have the doctors told you about Tripp?" He continued to watch Wendy.

Shandra glanced at Ryan. What Logan asked had perked him up.

"They were checking for internal bleeding. But no one has come to tell me what they've found." Wendy glanced toward a door just beyond the admittance desk.

Logan spun around and raised his chin in a motion that meant something to Ryan because he followed the

Tribal policeman to an area far enough away she and Wendy couldn't hear what they talked about.

"Why do you think Logan isn't acting like Logan?" Wendy asked.

"Could be someone is giving him flack about not solving Nelly's murder." Shandra wondered why she hadn't bumped into the FBI agent since their first meeting.

Ryan walked back over. "I gave Logan the note. He'll take it to Agent Tremaine. The FBI can run it through forensics quicker than the state police and it's their crime anyway."

"Do you want me to stay with you, Wendy?" Shandra asked, even though she could tell Ryan had something he wanted to tell her.

"No. You go. But could you wait until I change into my clothes? Then you can take my regalia back for me." Wendy stood and gathered her clothing.

"Yes, we can wait." Shandra noticed Logan was talking to the woman behind the admittance desk.

When Wendy disappeared down the hall, she turned to Ryan. "What has Logan practically steaming?"

"The lab here at the hospital determined there was more blood on the knife than Tripp's. There was also the same blood type as Nelly." Ryan glanced over her shoulder in the direction Logan had been.

"Really? That is the knife that killed Nelly?" The next thought that hit, made her stomach churn. "The killer was at the celebration dance."

"And tried to kill again." Ryan closed his mouth tight as Wendy returned.

She shoved her regalia into Shandra's arms.

"Thank you for taking these. Just drop them off at my house any time tomorrow." Her gaze landed on Shandra. "Oh! I'll need a ride home when I learn how Tripp's doing. There's not enough time for me to miss working on your dress."

It was getting late, but she had an idea. "I'll call Coop to bring my Jeep here. You can use it, and he can ride home with us."

"You don't mind me using your Jeep? I could call mother to come get me but…"

"I understand. It's no problem." Shandra pulled her phone out of her pocket and dialed Coop.

"Hey, how's Tripp doing?" he answered.

"We're not sure. No one has come out to tell us. I know it's getting late, but Wendy needs a vehicle. Could you bring my Jeep down here? We'll give you a lift back to the ranch." It was rare for Coop to turn her down when she made a request.

"If you don't mind if we stop by Sandy's cousin Ruby's to get her bags. Mom told her she could stay with us. The house is crowded but not nearly as crowded as Ruby's place. They are having a birthday party for her paternal grandmother and everyone has come to stay."

"That's fine." Shandra ended the conversation and turned to Wendy. "Coop's bringing the Jeep." She faced Ryan. "But we'll have to stop by Sandy's cousin's to get her bag." She smiled and shrugged.

Ryan barely heard what Shandra said, he was watching Logan, who still conversed with the woman at the admissions desk. "Sure, no problem." What was the officer thinking? He could tell Logan wasn't happy with Wendy's answers. And frankly, neither was he. If

Tripp could give them a better estimate of when the knife could have been taken out of his pickup it might help them narrow down the suspect pool. Right now, it was Wendy and Tripp. But it didn't make sense for them to stage such an elaborate way for the weapon to be found.

A hand waved in front of his face.

"Earth to Ryan," Shandra said.

"Sorry. I was bouncing around what ifs in my head." He reached out, drawing her toward him in a one-armed embrace.

"That's okay. I've been doing the same thing." She nodded toward the double doors at the end of the lobby. "Logan went in there. He's probably hoping to ask Tripp the same question he asked Wendy."

He nodded. "And possibly more if Tripp's up to it."

She led him over to two chairs. "We may as well sit here until Coop arrives."

Ryan didn't feel like sitting. He felt like taking a walk and thinking. "I think I'll go for a walk."

Shandra stood back up.

"You stay. I want to think and you'll be a distraction."

Her eyes narrowed.

"A good distraction but a distraction." He kissed her cheek and left through the emergency room automated doors. Once outside, he strode through the lit parking lot and onto the dark paved road that circled the whole building. He wanted a chance to talk to Logan again. Something was off about this whole thing. Duke was involved, he could feel it in his bones. However, he didn't believe the drug dealer stabbed Tripp. He'd only been in the wrong place at the wrong time and was pinched by someone who hated him.

Had Pim manipulated everyone? Had she given Wendy the note to make sure she and Tripp were off alone somewhere discussing it. Because he was pretty sure that was why the two were looking for some place quiet to talk. But how would she know where the two would go and get Duke to be in the same area? And did she have enough revenge in her heart to stab Tripp, a young man Shandra felt Pim still had feelings for? He'd made two trips around the grassy area and the medical center parking lot when he spotted Logan coming out the emergency doors.

He met the Tribal Officer at his patrol car.

"I wondered where you had gone." Logan said, leaning his butt on the hood of his car and crossing his arms.

"I was thinking. Did you get a chance to talk to Tripp?"

He nodded.

"When was the last time he'd seen that knife?" Ryan shoved his hands into his pants pockets.

"The Sunday before Nelly died. Said he'd shown it off after a Seven Drums service at the Community Center."

"Did you ask him if anyone saw him put it under his seat?"

"He said anyone who walked out to their cars could have seen him putting it away." Logan shoved away from the car and walked away several steps and back. "That is kind of a lame excuse. And I talked to the doctor on duty. He said the stab Tripp received barely punctured the peritoneum. Whoever did it was either weak or squeamish, or it was done for show."

"Not the same actions as the person who stabbed Nelly," Ryan said.

Logan nodded. "Which means, either Tripp is the murderer and he conned someone into knifing him to take the heat off him or someone found the knife and wanted to make it look like whoever killed Nelly wanted Tripp dead, too."

"This is either a crime of passion or revenge." Ryan spotted the Jeep's headlights pulling into the parking lot. "I'll ask more questions of the Elwoods and Sandy. There is a connection with something. Either drugs or relationships, that is the root of this crime."

"I agree. Tremaine is on the drug angle. He's been beating the bushes trying to get information that will pin this on Duke. Between you and me, he's going about it all wrong but refuses any help." Logan smiled for the first time since Wendy's scream. "I'm betting we figure this out before he does." He slapped Ryan on the shoulder as Shandra's copper Jeep pulled up beside the police vehicle.

Logan folded his body into the car as Coop jumped out of the Jeep.

"Did someone try to finish the job?" Coop asked.

"No. Just comparing notes." Ryan said, as Sandy joined them. "Let's take the keys to Wendy and gather Shandra."

They entered the lobby and found Shandra sitting by herself. She rose and walked over to them. "They allowed Wendy to go back and see Tripp." She put a hand on Coop's arm. "Thank you for driving here at such a late hour."

"I told you, we needed to make the drive to

Nespelem anyway." Coop smiled at Sandy.

"Leave the keys to the Jeep with the desk attendant and let's get going," Ryan said.

Coop and Sandy walked away and Shandra leaned closer to Ryan.

"What did you and Logan talk about?" she whispered.

"I'll tell you later. On the way home we need to ask your cousin and his girlfriend more about the love triangles involved in this murder."

She studied his face. "You mean, Nelly, Pim, Wendy, and Tripp?"

He nodded as Coop and Sandy rejoined them.

"Liz called while you were outside. She filled me in on Pim. While she's been acting strange… from what Liz said about her family and upbringing, I think she's just very needy for friendship and love." Shandra had gotten the same impression the times she'd had a conversation with the young woman.

"I'm not writing her off the list." Ryan started the vehicle as Coop opened the back door.

Coop and Sandy slid into the back seat. Shandra put her seatbelt on and sat sideways as they left the parking lot.

"I was wondering. Was Pim in love with Wesley Tibble?" Shandra asked the occupants of the back seat.

Ryan watched the two in his rearview mirror.

Sandy started to shake her head then stopped. "I'm not sure. I know she could get clingy with the guy she was dating. But love…" she glanced at Coop. "I'm not sure. They didn't go to parties at the lakes or socialize that way. Pim always held herself to a higher level than the rest of us."

Coop nodded. "If you went out with Pim, you couldn't drink or do drugs, and be prepared to be teased."

Ryan's interest piqued. "What do you mean by that?"

Coop shifted nervously and his gaze flit to Sandy and back to the rearview mirror. "She would talk like she had goods to share, if you know what I mean, then when a guy finally gave in and did her bidding to get those goods, she'd turn into an ice princess."

"And you know this how?" Sandy asked.

Chapter Twenty

"Andy had like a thirty-day infatuation with Pim when they were freshmen." Coop cringed. "Being the big brother, I had to listen to him and give advice."

Shandra found this information interesting. "What did Pim do when Andy called it off?"

Coop shrugged. "I don't think she did anything. I think she was using Andy to make Tripp jealous."

"And Tripp? Did he do Pim's bidding? Did he change his ways?" Shandra asked.

Sandy laughed. "Tripp was a junior. He had his pick of girls. We told you his reputation. He didn't change for Pim."

"Did she stay his girlfriend even though he didn't change?" Shandra had a feeling she knew the answer.

"She didn't go to the parties, so she didn't know he was." Coop put an arm around Sandy's shoulders. "On the weekends he'd party with Nelly and then during the week walk around school with Pim."

"Who had the longer relationship with Tripp? Pim

or Nelly?"

"Nelly," Sandy and Coop said in unison.

"And Wendy? Has she been with Tripp longer than Pim?" Shandra had a feeling the knife had been meant for Wendy.

"Wendy has been going out with Tripp longer than Pim ever did." Sandy nodded her head. "I think other than Tripp hanging out with Nelly at parties, Wendy has been the longest steady girlfriend Tripp has ever had."

"Yeah, now that you mention it," Coop added.

Ryan pulled into Nespelem. "Where am I going?"

Coop gave him directions to Ruby's house. Shandra remembered Sandy's cousin fondly. She had been helpful when they were proving Coop's innocence.

Ryan parked.

"I'll only be a minute," Sandy said, opening her door.

"I'll come with you. I haven't seen some of your relatives in a while." Coop slid out behind her and the two walked up to the door hand in hand.

Shandra smiled. "I like seeing them together. There was a time when I thought Coop's affection was one-sided."

"I remember," Ryan said, grasping her hand. "All this talk about high school drama has made me thankful I'm an adult."

Shandra laughed. "I didn't have any drama like that in my life as a high school student, but I watched a lot of scenes like they were talking about play out." She sobered and asked, "Do you think Pim killed Nelly and tonight was trying for Wendy and missed?"

Ryan played with her fingers and didn't say anything for a long time. "I'm not sure what to think. There are several scenarios, I can think of. Logan found out Tripp showed that knife off at services on Sunday. He didn't say how many people or who they were. But it was at the Community Center."

"That means we still have a lot of suspects, even if we rule out who we've been questioning." She sighed. "I keep thinking there is something we're missing. Some small detail that will make things clear."

Ryan nodded. "That's usually the way it is."

Coop and Sandy exited the house, a suitcase in Coop's hand.

"I'm ready to get back to your aunt's and get some sleep," Ryan said, as the two entered the pickup.

"That sounds good to us," Coop said, closing the door.

~*~

The dancers swirled, mixing colors. Drums boomed and voices wailed. In the middle of the dancers stood what appeared to be a family. A child, man, and woman. Their faces were painted, making it hard to see who they were. Dancers grabbed the child. Shandra couldn't tell if the child was a boy or a girl. The child cried and reached back to the adults. The mother stretched her arms and another group of dancers drew her away. Soon the child and woman had been swallowed up in the dancers. All that remained was the man on his knees in the open circle, his face in his hands as if he were crying.

Shandra woke. Her heart heavy. The man had appeared to be in complete despair. She glanced at the clock on the bedside table. 3 A.M.

Her mind kept conjuring up the vision of the man. It was evident she wasn't going to get any more sleep. Shandra slipped out of bed, grabbed her purse, and tried to descend the old creaky stairs without waking anyone.

In the kitchen, she filled the tea kettle and set it to heating, before sitting at the table and pulling out the small notebook and pen in her purse. The woman and child in her dream had to be Nelly and Fawn. She didn't know of anyone else with a child who was involved in the case. Who was the man? If Fawn's father hadn't come forward by now to claim her, why would he be feeling despair over her loss and Nelly's death?

The kettle started to whistle.

Shandra jumped up to stop the sound and bumped into Ryan, reaching for the whistling kettle.

"Did I wake you?" she asked, grabbing cups.

"I woke up and saw you were gone. I figured you either had a dream or you were obsessing over the murder." He poured hot water in the two cups and placed the kettle on a cold burner.

Shandra dropped tea bags in each cup. "Both. I did have a dream and couldn't go back to sleep. Now I'm trying to make sense of what we know and what the dream meant."

They sat sipping the hot tea as she told Ryan about the dream. "But no one has seemed to care that Aunt Jo and Uncle Martin took in Fawn." She stared into Ryan's dark eyes. "I'm beginning to think this doesn't have anything to do with Fawn's father. It's someone else's."

Ryan nodded once. "I'm curious to find out who stabbed Tripp. From what we've discovered from Coop and Sandy, Nelly and Tripp were a couple where people partied. Could someone have thought they were more of a couple than they were and tried to get revenge on Tripp by killing Nelly, then found out he didn't care?"

Shandra shook her head. "The love on Pim's face when she looked at Tripp tonight after the stabbing, and the way she and Wendy acted toward each other…I think Tripp wasn't the victim. I think Pim is getting rid of her competition." The vision of the man in despair flickered in her mind. "But that doesn't work with the dream I had."

Ryan drained his tea cup. "We can go round and round all night with what ifs. Let's get a couple more hours of sleep and get the facts from Logan in the morning." He picked up her cup and placed them both in the sink.

Shandra stood. It made sense. Hopefully, she could fall back to sleep.

~*~

Ryan went for a walk while Shandra and her aunt made breakfast. He wandered to the area where the celebration dance had happened. He retraced the path he'd witnessed Duke take. The drug dealer's appearance may have been legit, but Duke had no reason to come to the celebration. Unless it was to see what had been found out about Nelly's killer and see if he was on the top of the suspect list. Or to meet one of his runners. Why had he been near Tripp and Wendy? Was Tripp a dealer? Was he also trying to quit like Nelly had tried? Ryan pulled out his phone and scrolled through the new emails his friend in the FBI had sent him.

It appeared the knife Logan confiscated last night had Nelly's blood on it and had been identified as the weapon that killed Nelly. The only partial prints matched Tripp and Wendy. Which made sense since Wendy made the knife and Tripp owned it. But for there to be only their fingerprints, the assailant had worn gloves.

He thought back. It was warm last night. Anyone with gloves on would have been noticed. Duke hadn't worn any. His fancy ring had glinted in the firelight. Ryan headed back to the house to ask if anyone had seen someone with gloves on.

Andy wandered out of the barn, rubbing his eyes and blinking at the sun.

"You're getting up a bit late for a farm boy," Ryan joked.

Andy blinked and peered at him. "I had a few too many with some of my friends last night after we cleaned up."

Ryan nodded. "Coffee, and I'm sure breakfast, is ready by now." They'd walked several steps when he asked, "Did you see anyone wearing gloves last night?"

Andy stopped and stared at him. "All of us who were handling the wood."

"Was there anyone besides you, me, and Coop?"

"Old Moses and our cousins, Jared and Willie." Andy swiped a hand across his forehead. "That's all I remember. But I didn't help load up the leftover wood when we cleaned up."

"Why?"

"I couldn't find my gloves and decided to join my friends." Andy shrugged.

That left one pair of gloves that someone, like the assailant, could have grabbed and used. But how would they have known there would be gloves available?

"Do the people who handle the wood always wear gloves?"

Andy looked at him as if he'd asked something silly. "Yeah, why?"

"Nothing." He didn't want to go into all of it with the young man. He resumed walking.

Jo opened the screen. "Good. I was going to send Martin to get the two of you if I didn't see you."

Ryan entered the kitchen, inhaling the smells of ham and biscuits he remembered as a child. His mother always made large breakfasts to feed her hungry family and hardworking husband.

Shandra motioned to a chair next to her. The table was laden with ham, biscuits, scrambled eggs, and fruit.

They sat elbow to elbow. Sandy was on Shandra's right with Coop to her right at the end of
the table. Martin sat at the head of the table with Andy to his left, then Fawn and Jo.

Ryan waited until everyone had dug in and were just picking at the bits left on their plates to ask, "Did you see anyone besides the men who handled the wood last night wearing gloves?"

Chapter Twenty-one

Shandra had a hard time not spinning toward Ryan. He had found out something while he was outside walking around. Instead, she studied her family, all thinking.

"I don't remember seeing anyone," she said to start the conversation.

"I told you what I knew," Andy said.

Jo shook her head.

Martin looked around the table. "The only ones I saw were the wood crew. These two, Old Moses, Jared, Will, and you."

"Why was Old Moses on the wood crew? Is he family?" Shandra asked, wondering why no one had said anything about that.

"No, he's not blood family but he is a part of the community with all his work at the center," Jo said.

"He always helps out with community events, like a celebration." Uncle Martin studied Ryan. "Why are you asking about gloves?"

Shandra didn't miss Ryan's quick glance at Fawn who appeared to be ignoring the conversation.

"The knife that was dropped last night had only Tripp and Wendy's fingerprints on it." He glanced at Shandra.

She understood what he was saying. It was the same knife used to kill Nelly, but he didn't want to say anything with Fawn in the room.

"And Wendy wouldn't stab Tripp and Tripp wouldn't stab himself," Sandy said. "That means whoever stabbed him had to be wearing gloves."

"And the knife had been used before." Ryan glanced at the child and everyone else at the table nodded.

She was glad her family was smart enough to realize the meaning of Ryan's statement and actions.

"You think the same person tried to kil-harm Tripp?" Aunt Jo asked, watching Fawn.

Ryan shrugged. "I'm not sure. Shandra has another thought on that. I'm still trying to figure out why Du-Waters was here."

Shandra smiled at Ryan for realizing the girl would know the man's first name but probably not his last.

"We know Andy invited him—"

Uncle Martin cut in. "Why did you do that?" He glared at his son.

Andy shrunk back in his seat as he sipped a cup of coffee. He hadn't added any food to his plate. "I knew Ryan and Shandra were interested in him. Thought they could catch him at something."

"But here?" Martin glanced at Fawn and back at his son.

"I know. I wasn't thinking." Andy dropped his chin to his chest.

"I wish someone could give me a clear rundown of who all he talked with," Ryan said.

Andy perked up. "You could ask Samuel Red Cloud. He's one of the rez cops. He was here just to keep an eye on Du-Waters."

"How do you know this?" Shandra asked, wondering how her cousin, who she was pretty sure wasn't involved in drugs in any way, could know so much.

"His brother, Dan, was one of the guys I partied with last night." He glanced sheepishly at his parents. "He said his brother wasn't dressed as if on duty but he'd been told to keep an eye on…" He glanced toward Fawn. "You know who."

Ryan stood. "That means Logan should be able to fill me in." He strode out the door pulling his phone out of the holster on his belt.

Shandra glanced around the table at her family. "Thank you for the celebration dance last night. It was thoughtful and helped me learn more about my heritage."

"I'm sorry it ended the way it did," Aunt Jo said.

"You couldn't help that."

Sandy stood. "Fawn, I'd love to see your pony, Princess."

The little girl hopped off her chair. "She come to me."

Coop started to stand.

"Stay here and visit with your family. Shandra might have questions you can answer," Sandy said, taking Fawn's hand.

"Thank you," Shandra said, realizing the young woman was taking the child away so they could really talk about what had happened.

"This has to be cleared up before your wedding. It's a bad omen to have something like this hanging over the family." Sandy led the little girl out the back door.

"That's a smart woman you're going to marry," Uncle Martin said, putting a hand on his oldest son's shoulder.

"Thanks, Dad. She is." Coop turned his attention to Shandra. "The knife that was used on Tripp is the same knife that killed Nelly?"

She nodded. No sense denying it. Her family knew to keep the information among them.

"I can't believe a killer was at the celebration dance." Aunt Jo said. "And I agree, we have to clear this up before your wedding."

Shandra studied her family. Up till now, Ryan had been the only person she told her dreams to. However, it seemed like they would be able to help her with their knowledge of the people who lived on the reservation.

"I had a dream last night…"

They all leaned in to listen and she retold the dream.

"The man, woman, and child, to me represent Nelly, Fawn, and Fawn's father," she said.

Aunt Jo shook her head. "That doesn't make sense. Her father has never come forward. Never tried to claim her. I can't see him being upset over losing her or Nelly."

"Excuse me." Andy bolted out of his chair and headed to the bathroom under the stairs.

Shandra did quick calculations of the information she'd gathered. She peered at Coop. Andy was an adult now at twenty-one. "From the history I've been told, and Andy's own account, along with the father having a conscience by putting money in a mailbox every month, I believe you may have taken in your granddaughter," she said, shifting her gaze to Jo and Martin.

Jo gasped and Martin's brows bunched together in a frown.

"Are you saying…" Coop glanced toward the bathroom door, "Andy is Fawn's father?"

She shrugged. "It's the only thing that makes sense. And that would also mean that the man in my dream isn't Andy, the child isn't Fawn, and the woman isn't Nelly."

Martin started to stand, but Jo's hand on his arm settled him back in his chair. "Coop, go see if your brother is ready to come tell us the truth."

Coop rose, glanced at Shandra, and walked over to the bathroom door. He rapped twice, said something softly, and entered the room.

"I can't believe he hasn't said anything," Jo said, peering into her husband's eyes. "Especially after Fawn came to stay with us. But you know, I kept seeing little things about her that looked familiar. This would explain what I was seeing."

Shandra rose. "I'll let you talk about this as a family."

"You are part of this family," Jo said.

Coop and Andy entered the kitchen.

"But this is something you need to discuss without me." She stepped out the back door and scanned the area for Ryan. He stood over by the corral, his cell phone to his ear.

She sauntered over to him, still wrapping her mind around the fact her twenty-one-year-old cousin was a father.

"I understand I'm not part of this investigation, but I have a lot at stake." Ryan reached out, putting an arm around Shandra's shoulders. If this murder didn't get cleared up, he had a feeling his wedding would be postponed and that wasn't going to happen if he could help it. Logan hadn't answered his phone and when he'd asked to talk to Officer Red Cloud he'd been getting stonewalled.

"I'm sorry, but we can't give out that information." The line went silent.

He growled and shoved his phone into his belt holster.

"I can't believe Logan wouldn't talk to you," Shandra said.

"It wasn't Logan. He didn't answer his phone. Dispatch wouldn't put me through to the officer who had followed Duke." He'd noticed her furrowed brow and her slow steps as she'd walked over to him. "What's going on in there?" He tipped his head toward the house.

"I told them what I'd uncovered while trying to find Nelly's killer." She sighed.

"And?"

"Andy is Fawn's father."

He released her and stared into her eyes. "How did you figure that out?"

"I pieced together things people said and it just made sense. I didn't stick around to see if he denies it."

Ryan whistled low. "You are not going to be his

favorite cousin."

"I know, but Jo and Martin had a right to know they wouldn't have to worry about Duke trying to take away Fawn. Her father is right here."

"True. If it wasn't Duke, Nelly and Fawn in your dream…"

She shook her head. "I don't know who it was. But it has to be something connected to drugs."

"Why do you say that?" He studied her.

"Because Nelly, Duke, and I'm thinking Tripp, are or have been involved in the drug scene on the reservation." She glanced at his phone. "Try Logan again. If he doesn't answer, we need to talk to Tripp."

Ryan dialed Officer Logan Rider again. The phone rang.

"Rider," said an out of breath Logan.

"This is Ryan. Shandra and I would like to meet up with you if that's possible."

"I'm just returning to Nespelem. Duke Waters was run off the road when he left the police station early this morning."

"Is he alive?" Ryan held up a hand as Shandra opened her mouth.

"Barely. They took him to the Coulee Medical Center." A car door slammed. "I can meet you in Nespelem at my grandmother's."

"We'll be there." Ryan slipped his phone into the holster and grasped Shandra's elbow. "Go get your purse and we'll meet Logan at his grandmother's."

"Who?"

She didn't have to say more. He knew what she wanted to know. "Duke Waters. He's still alive." Ryan told her what Logan had said.

"I'll be right back." Shandra jogged to the house.

Sandy stepped out of the barn leading Princess with Fawn on her back.

"It's a good day for a horseback ride," Ryan said.

Before Sandy could reply, Andy and Coop arrived. Andy took the lead rope from Sandy as Coop led her away from the young man and his daughter.

Ryan walked to his pickup as Shandra exited the house. She hurried over to him.

"I told Jo we'd be gone for a while. I didn't tell her anything else," she said, sliding into the passenger seat.

He nodded toward Andy leading the horse. "How is everyone doing?"

"The little time I had, Jo said Andy had planned to tell them, just knew how so many felt about Nelly and didn't want them thinking bad about him. He'd figured it out when Fawn was born."

Ryan started the vehicle and drove away from the ranch. "That's why there was money in the mailbox every month. Did he say if Nelly mentioned it to him?"

"I'm not sure. Didn't have enough time to ask." Shandra buckled and faced him. "Did Logan say anything else?"

"Like if they had a suspect?"

"Yes."

"No. Nothing else." He glanced over at her before taking the turn onto the county road. "He could have been tired and ran off the road."

"Do you really believe that?" she asked.

"No. Not if you are thinking this had to do with drugs. If you think about it. Nelly seduced young men into starting drugs for Duke. Duke supplied the drugs, and if Tripp was a target, he could have been a dealer.

That could make the homicide and the attempts revenge killings."

Chapter Twenty-two

Shandra smiled and allowed Mrs. Rider to seat
them and pour coffee for the men and tea for her before
she focused on Logan. "Was Duke losing control of his
car an accident?"

The big officer shook his head. "Definite marks of
someone forcing him off the road. He's lucky he's still
alive."

"Did the chief send anyone over to keep an eye on
Tripp?" Ryan asked.

Logan stared at him. "You think there will be
another attempt at him?"

"This has to be drug related. Is or was Tripp a
dealer?" Ryan asked.

Shandra glanced at Mrs. Rider. Her lips were
pursed and her head moved back and forth in short
movements. She didn't like the talk of drugs and death
in her home.

Logan peered at Shandra and then Ryan. "No one
is supposed to know, but Tripp has been the Feds

informant. He's working for the Feds, not Duke. Though his cover is a dealer."

Shandra stared at Logan. "His flings with Nelly at the parties were to gather information, weren't they?"

He nodded. "I can't say how far he went, but he was to get close to her to find out all he could about the operation and Duke. After he started dating Wendy, he wanted to quit, but the Feds are as bad as the drug lords, they don't like to let anyone go that knows anything."

"But someone who didn't know he was an informant would think he's part of the drug problem," Shandra said. Which would explain the attack on him. And the need to keep him safe.

"Another reason to have a guard on his room. If not the tribal police the FBI should for sure," Ryan said.

Logan stood. "I'll make that call and be right back." He strode from the room, ducking at the kitchen door.

Shandra put a hand on Mrs. Rider's. "I'm sorry to bring this kind of talk into your home."

The old woman patted her hand with a gnarled one. "We have to clean up this reservation and make the young people realize they can change the cycle of addiction."

"I agree. That is what my scholarship is about. Helping young women realize there is more to life than drinking, drugs, and being a victim." Shandra studied the old woman's rheumy eyes. She sensed a strength in their depths and knowledge that times could be better.

"It is good what you are doing. It could have turned out better had Fawn's father stepped forward."

Shandra studied the woman. She *had* known all along who the father was. "Grandmother knew Andy was Fawn's father."

Mrs. Rider nodded. "She believed Andy would come forward when he had matured and understood how important a father is to a child."

"Did she talk to him? Or Aunt Jo?" Shandra wondered at how her grandmother could keep something like this from her daughter. Especially, knowing her daughter craved a female child.

"She only confided in me. Saying the truth would come out when it was needed." She picked up her coffee cup. "Now is the time with the mother gone."

Shandra agreed. "Do you have an insight into who we are looking for?"

"No. Only that you know. Your grandmother told me you know. You just have to stop trying so hard."

"That's what I tell her. She tries to make things more complicated than they are." Ryan leaned forward.

Shandra jumped at his voice. She'd forgotten he was still in the room as she'd talked with Mrs. Rider.

Logan strode back into the kitchen and took his seat. "They are sending someone to watch over Tripp. Duke isn't going to make it."

While she didn't care for the man and what he stood for, no one deserved to die before they lived to an old age. "Any idea who forced him off the road?"

"There were no witnesses to the accident. The scrapes on Duke's vehicle were gray, like primer."

Ryan shook his head. "That could be half the vehicles on this reservation."

"I know. But one of them will also have red stripes on their right front fender or bumper. Duke was driving a bright red convertible."

Shandra had a horrible thought. "Did Duke have

any passengers?"

Logan stared at her. "None that we found, why? Do you know something?"

"No. When you said convertible I had the strange feeling someone had been thrown from the vehicle."

"That would have been Duke. He didn't have his seatbelt on. When the car hit the tree, he was thrown forward."

She shuddered and had the odd sensation she'd been with the person who watched him slam into the tree.

"Shandra? Honey, you look pale," Ryan said, grasping her hand.

"I'm okay. Just…"

Mrs. Rider grasped her other hand and squeezed. It was as if Ella were telling her the thoughts and visions were okay.

She glanced at the woman and smiled at Ryan. "I'm fine."

"It will take a couple days before we get any information back from forensics about the crash." Logan drained his cup and stood. "I have to get back to work."

Ryan waved a hand toward Shandra. "Is there any chance we could talk with Officer Red Cloud to see who Duke spoke to last night?"

"I'll see what I can do, but I can't make any promises. His butt will be kicked all the way to the Canadian Border if the chief finds out he's told you anything."

"We understand." Ryan stood and shook the tribal police officer's hand. "We appreciate you keeping us in the loop. As has been stated by several people in

Shandra's family, we need this cleared up before the wedding."

"Yes. It would bring bad spirits to have a wedding when so many are grieving," Mrs. Rider said.

Shandra gave the woman a hug. "Thank you for everything."

"My pleasure. Remember, don't doubt your dreams and feelings. Let the answers come. Don't chase them."

"I'll remember." Shandra followed Ryan out the front door and watched Logan get into his police vehicle.

Ryan faced her. "Now what? We don't need to see Tripp because we know why he is involved. And we can't talk to Officer Red Cloud until he contacts us."

Shandra grinned. "Won't it fry Velma when she discovers that Tripp has been on the side of good all this time and she's been thinking him bad?"

Ryan laughed. "I would almost pay to see her face when the truth comes out."

Dream a Little Dream, floated from the depths of her purse. She dug out her phone.

Velma.

"Hello?"

"I'm headed to the Community Center for services. It would be good if you sat in on them."

"Can Ryan come?"

"If he wants, but it would be better for you to immerse yourself if he wasn't present."

She understood what her aunt was saying. She'd be wondering what he thought and felt rather than letting the experience fill her.

Shandra glanced at Ryan. "Can you find something to do if I attend a Seven Drums service at the

Community Center?"

He nodded and headed to the pickup.

"I can do that. See you soon." She dropped her phone into her bag and followed Ryan.

Inside, he asked, "Who invited you?"

"Velma." She buckled up as he pulled away from the curb.

"She didn't want me to attend?"

"Not that you shouldn't but that I'd be more immersed if you weren't there."

Ryan laughed. "She thinks I'd be able to keep your mind off something you've been wanting to learn the last three years? She must think my power over you is stronger than it is."

Shandra shook her head. "She's just worried you will keep me from learning. That you'll think my discovering my heritage takes up too much of my time."

"Doesn't she realize I want you to find your roots? Why else would I be going along with the wedding here at the reservation and following so many of the traditions?" Ryan thought her family understood he would never take her away from them. He wasn't like her stepfather and mother.

"I'm sure your vows will show them how you feel."

Ryan grimaced. He wasn't good with putting how he felt into words. "Are we writing our own vows?"

"I'm writing mine the traditional way. All you have to do is promise to never stray or hurt me." She clasped her hand with his. "Oh, and to make Velma happy, you won't make me choose between you and my family."

"That's a given." He put the vehicle in park at the

stop sign and leaned over, kissing her.

A car behind them honked.

Ryan straightened and drove onto the highway, headed toward the agency.

"What are you going to do while I'm with Velma?" Shandra asked.

"I'm not sure. Maybe drive toward Omak and see what they are finding at the wreck site. I won't go to Coulee Medical Center. It sounds like Duke wouldn't be in any shape to tell me anything anyway." He also thought he might just cruise around and check any primer gray vehicles for red streaks.

"Do you think whoever is doing this will go after Tripp again?"

He glanced at Shandra. Her gaze was forward and she worried her bottom lip. "He'll be fine. He has the FBI guarding him. I'm thinking whoever is doing this is an amateur. Otherwise, Tripp would be in the morgue and not a hospital room." He thought a moment. "Whoever it is, was lucky with the attack on Nelly. That probably gave them confidence to go after Tripp the same way. Only it didn't work because there was a crowd and the knife didn't go in far enough because of his haste. With Nelly, it was just the two of them and he had all the time he needed."

"I need to stop thinking about this. That's what Mrs. Rider told me. Let it go and the answers will come." Shandra started unbuckling her seatbelt as he pulled into the Community Center parking lot.

Ryan put the pickup in park and leaned toward her. He grasped her chin and peered into her eyes. "Think only about learning more about your heritage and our wedding. Don't let any of this dampen your happiness."

"That's what I plan to do." She kissed him quick and slipped out of the vehicle.

He watched her walk into the building before pulling out of the parking lot. A quick glance at the gas gauge and he realized he needed fuel. The Trading Post was across the highway from the Community Center.

That would be a good place to get fueled up and maybe ask about a primer colored vehicle.

Chapter Twenty-three

The Community Center was busy. Shandra hadn't realized how many on the reservation followed the Seven Drum religion.

Stopping inside the main doors, she spotted Velma. She dodged the people coming into the building and stopped beside her aunt. "I didn't realize there would be so many people here."

Velma peered down at her. "With the Long House burned down and not replaced this is where we hold our *Walahsat* services." She glanced at the ramp down to the basketball court.

Shandra followed Velma and the others down onto the court. Chairs were lined up on the north and south sides of the room. The women sat in chairs on the south side and the men on the north side. The drummers were set up on the west side.

Velma walked over to the women's side and took a seat beside Wendy, leaving one on her other side for Shandra.

She wondered if her cousin had left Tripp's side to come and pray for him or if her mother had insisted.

Before she could sit, a bell rang.

"Spin counter clockwise," Velma whispered.

Those that had been sitting rose and everyone spun counter clockwise once and sat.

An elderly man who appeared to be the leader, spoke in the old language, rang the bell, and everyone began to sing.

Shandra listened to the words, though she had no understanding of them, and let her mind and heart drift along on the beat of the drum.

~*~

Ryan was headed north on the highway to find the spot where Duke went off the road, when his phone buzzed. He pulled over when he didn't recognize the number.

"Greer," he answered.

"This is Officer Red Cloud. Logan said you had some questions for me?" His tone sounded skeptical.

"What did Logan tell you about me?" He didn't want the man to get into trouble for giving out police information.

"That you were going to marry Shandra Higheagle and you were a county detective." The sound of shuffling papers came through the phone. "But I couldn't find you listed on any of the counties around here."

"I'm from Weippe County in Idaho. I don't want to get you into trouble, but I'm curious about who Duke talked to during the celebration party at the Higheagle Ranch on Saturday night."

"You want this cleared up to not interfere with

your wedding." The man's voice held an aha of recognition of why the information was important to Ryan.

"Yes. I thought, being from somewhere else, I might have a different opinion of what might have transpired between Duke and those he talked with." He didn't want the man to think he was some cop who horned in on others jurisdictions.

"I see. Well, I can't talk to you about it here. Meet me in twenty minutes in the Trading Post parking lot."

"I'll be there." Ryan put his phone away and did a U-turn.

~*~

Shandra didn't understand the words the elderly man chanted, but she repeated the words along with the others present. After several songs, one by one people stood up and walked to the center of the room.

They told stories of loss, determination, and faith. As each one told their story, Shandra better understood the lives of the people on the reservation.

One man, not much older than Shandra, stood and began his story. "It stabbed my heart to…"

His voice faded as another person came to mind. "Nelly Bingham's been stabbed."

Shandra shot to her feet.

Velma grasped her arm, drawing her back to her seat. "You don't interrupt while someone is telling their story."

Shandra nodded but her mind was going back over the events she knew. When she and Velma had come upon the body there was no way to tell Nelly had been stabbed. How had Old Moses known? If she had still been on her feet or knees, surely, he would have helped her, not come to the office to have someone call the police. He worked here and could have seen Tripp showing off the knife Wendy made him. He could have witnessed Tripp putting the knife under the seat in his pickup.

How did Old Moses lure Nelly to the sweat lodge and why?

The man was still telling his story. Everyone but her seemed absorbed in what he was saying.

Shandra ached to ask Velma about Old Moses but knew she would learn nothing until the man had finished his story.

~*~

Ryan and Officer Red Cloud sat on Ryan's tailgate in the back parking lot of the Trading Post.

"You were assigned to follow Duke at the celebration the other night," Ryan started. "Who all did he talk with?"

The officer pulled out his notepad. "When he was standing by himself, I'd jot down who he'd just talked to." He flipped the pages and read, "Tripp confronted him when he first arrived. I could tell he wasn't happy Duke was there."

Ryan knew why. Having the drug lord at a celebration held by the family he wanted to join wouldn't win him any brownie points with Velma.

"Then he meandered, talking to some of the younger women. Looked like he was flirting and they weren't going for it." Samuel grinned. "He talked to two males who we believe are dealing for him. But no money or substances exchanged." He flipped the page. "Duke had words with Old Moses by the wood pile when the dancing started. Then it was like Duke searched the crowd and spotted Tripp and Wendy making a break away from the crowd. He caught up to Tripp said something to him and moved on. My eyes were on Duke when Wendy cried out. That's when I saw Tripp was bleeding." He glanced up from the notepad. "As much as I'd like to say Duke stabbed Tripp, he didn't. It happened after he'd walked away."

"Do you remember anyone who was in the vicinity who you thought was odd?" The killer had to still be in the area when Wendy cried out. Everyone would have noticed someone hurrying away.

Samuel shook his head, then stopped. "Old Moses. He was standing with his back to the scene."

Ryan's attention snapped on the officer. "What is his last name?"

"Tibble."

"As in Wesley Tibble?"

"Yeah, Old Moses is Wesley's father. Shame how Wesley drowned in the lake." Samuel's gaze had drifted to the parking lot. It snapped back to Ryan. "Do you think he's doing this for revenge?"

"Oldest reason in the world for killing someone. Where would he be right now?" Ryan hopped off the tail gate and pulled out his phone.

"The Seven Drums services are being held right now. He'll go to the Community Center when it's over to put the chairs away." Officer Red Cloud stood with his hand on his radio transmitter. "I'll call in our suspicions to the chief."

Ryan nodded. Shandra was at the Community Center. He didn't want her confronting Old Moses. The man had killed twice and attempted a third, he didn't like the odds of Shandra becoming number four.

Chapter Twenty-four

There were two more who stood up and spoke. A quick glance at the clock on the gymnasium wall said it was nearing noon. Shandra had never been to such a long church service.

When no one else stood and the elder rang his bell signaling another song, Shandra grabbed Velma's sleeve and pulled her out the nearest door. It happened to be on the downward side of the building, facing the sweat lodge.

"What are you dragging me out here for?" Velma accused.

"What is Old Moses' last name?" She had to find the reason for him to go after Nelly, Duke, and Tripp.

"Tibble. Why couldn't that wait until after the services?" Velma placed her fisted hands on her ample hips and glared.

Tibble! "Any relation to Wesley?"

"His father. Why?" Velma's glare had softened into interest.

"Remember the day he came to the office and said Nelly had been stabbed?"

"Yeah, but I'd rather forget it." Velma's nose scrunched in distaste.

"When we walked down to the sweat lodge, could you tell if she'd been stabbed?" Shandra asked. Velma had to see what she'd discovered.

Her aunt stared up at the sky and shook her head. "No."

"Then how do you think Old Moses knew?" She peered at her aunt like a parent waiting for a child to spit out the correct answer.

"You have to be wrong. He's never even thrown litter out a window," Velma said.

The sound of an engine coming around the side of the building caught her attention. A dark green fender, followed by the body of an older pickup came into view.

"That's Old Moses," Velma whispered, grabbing her arm to haul her back into the building.

"You go and call Ryan. Tell him what I think." Shandra wasn't afraid of the man. He'd killed the others because they had harmed his son. She hadn't even known his son.

"He's not going to like this," Velma said, disappearing into the building.

"Miss Shandra, what are you doing out here?" Old Moses asked, stepping out of the vehicle and coming around the front toward her.

"I was falling asleep and wanted some fresh air." She waved a hand toward the door.

He cocked his head. "You left a service before it finished?"

Not knowing how much he knew about the service she said, "I waited until all the stories were told and they started singing again. I'm afraid not knowing the language, I'm at a disadvantage of knowing what they are singing about."

He smiled. "The songs are about how the earth nurtures us and the animals sustain us. Hasn't Velma taught you what the Seven Drums religion is about?"

"Only bits and pieces. We aren't together enough for her to have taught me as much as I would like to learn." She nodded to the sweat lodge. "Has the area around the sweat lodge been purified?"

He didn't glance that direction. His gaze remained on her. "Why do you ask?"

"Aunt Jo said Ryan and I had to do a purification sweat before the wedding. I was just making sure we won't have to postpone the wedding."

His shoulders relaxed. "Your aunt can perform the purification ritual. You should talk to her."

"Aunt Velma?" She found it odd her aunt hadn't mentioned it to her.

He nodded. "She performed the ritual after Wesley was killed in the lake. No one could swim or fish until she had."

"Wesley? Was that a son?" She wanted to keep him talking until Ryan arrived. And maybe she could also get him to confess.

"My only son. He was a good boy. He and Pim were talking about getting married. But he'd fallen for Nelly's wicked ways." The older man's eyes narrowed and hatred surged in their dark depths.

"I don't understand?" She shook her head, hoping she appeared as lost as she was faking.

He turned the hatred on her. "How could you give someone with such evil in her heart a means to leave this place?"

Shandra took a step back. "I don't know what you're talking about."

"The scholarship. You were giving her a ticket out of here. She didn't deserve it. There are so many other young women who don't prey on young men's hormones that should have received it. Not that whore." This Old Moses was nothing like the old man who shuffled his feet and barely said anything.

"I didn't know all of this about her." Shandra held up her hands submissively.

"Velma knew. She should have warned you."

"She did in a way, but I thought what she said was just because she didn't like Nelly, not because she was really a bad person."

Sirens sounded in the distance.

Old Moses heard it too. He hurried into his pickup and backed it up.

Shandra didn't know whether to follow him or go into the building. Before the vehicle started forward, it had two tribal police cars in front of it.

Old Moses put his head on the steering wheel.

Logan sprang out of one police vehicle and another tribal policeman and Ryan leaped out of the other car. The tribal policemen went after Old Moses.

Ryan sprinted over to her. "Are you okay? Did he hurt you?"

She shook her head. "He wouldn't hurt me. I didn't hurt his son. I feel sorry for him. He could have handled things differently. Murder will put him in jail."

"When people are seeking revenge, they don't

think about what will happen after they have their revenge." Ryan held her tight.

"Why were you with a tribal policeman?"

"That is Samuel Red Cloud. When he told me who Duke talked to at the celebration and that he'd witnessed Old Moses near Tripp, I asked him Moses's last name." Ryan released her and clasped a hand, leading her around the building.

"Tibbles," she said.

"Yes. Samuel remembered Wesley had a pickup he'd been working on when he died. We went to the Tibble residence and found a primer gray pickup with red streaks on the right front fender. Samuel had just called it in when Velma called me."

"How did Logan get here so fast?" Shandra asked as they climbed the short ascent to the front of the building.

"He'd had a conversation with Tripp, without Wendy around, and discovered that Old Moses had threatened him after Wesley died. Saying he knew that Tripp had given his boy the drugs that caused him to drown." Ryan scanned the parking lot. "We need a lift to my pickup so we can go home."

She nodded. "Here comes Velma."

~*~

Shandra had her bag packed and stood on the back porch with Aunt Jo, waiting for Ryan to get off the phone. "Be sure to give that scholarship packet to Pim. I want her to be able to get registered for the fall term."

"I'm sure Velma will see to it. That is if she can get over the fact she didn't know Tripp at all." Jo laughed and Shandra joined in. When Velma had discovered Tripp wasn't a drug dealer, she went into hiding for several hours.

"I'm glad you discovered who Fawn's father is," Aunt Jo said, watching Andy and Fawn riding horses in the corral.

"I'm glad he took responsibility for her when she was born by giving Nelly money. And I understand Nelly hoping one day Duke would give in and say Fawn was his and marry her." Shandra did understand that Nelly had been so besotted with Duke that she had built up a fairytale of sorts about how he would come to his senses and love her and Fawn.

"What saddens me is that no one realized how much anger Old Moses had stored up since Wesley's death and his wife committing suicide." Jo hugged her arms to her body. "It's scary to know anyone could break and do such a horrific thing as kill another person."

"I know. Having been involved with Ryan and several murders, I'm becoming nearly as cynical as he is." Shandra watched Ryan stroll toward them, putting his phone away.

"What did Logan have to say?" she asked when he stopped at the porch.

"Tibble admitted he told Nelly that Duke wanted to meet her by the sweat lodge. He knew that was the one person she'd do anything to meet. He'd taken the knife from Tripp's pickup to scare her into telling him who all had taken part in killing his son. When she'd just laughed at him and told him he was crazy, he snapped and stabbed her."

"But he didn't have any blood on him," Shandra said.

"He went to his truck, drove home, changed, and

then came back and walked into the office." Ryan shook his head. "The time difference is my fault. I never did ask the time of death."

"And Tripp?"

"He figured since he and Nelly were always seen partying, that Tripp had to have something to do with Wesley getting hooked on drugs. But without confronting Tripp and getting his anger up, he attempted to stab him, only to have his conscience not go through with it." Ryan picked up her bag. "When he couldn't go through with Tripp's stabbing, he worked himself up that it was all Duke's fault and he should be the one to die. He pulled Wesley's vehicle out of the garage and waited for Duke to leave the police station. He said with Duke gone he was at peace."

Shandra shook her head. "He'll never be at peace with all that on his conscience."

"I agree." Aunt Jo hugged her. "See you in two weeks."

Chapter Twenty-five

Shandra stood inside the women's teepee on the
Higheagle Ranch. It had taken some persuasion to talk
her aunt and uncle into allowing the wedding to happen
on the ranch. She didn't want it at the Community
Center after experiencing the celebration here in May.

They had finally agreed when Velma said she
would officiate only if the wedding were on the ranch.

"How are you feeling?" Sandy asked, helping
Shandra into the beautiful white doeskin dress Wendy
had made for her. It was decorated with elk teeth and
glass beads.

"Surreal." Shandra hadn't stopped grinning from
her first step into the teepee. Aunt Jo, Wendy, and
Sandy had agreed to help her prepare. Coop, Conor, and
Uncle Martin were in the men's teepee with Ryan. He
would need less help since he was wearing his usual
western attire. But she realized they were there for
moral support as he waited for her to get ready.

"You are beautiful. Mother would be so proud to

see you right now." Aunt Jo dabbed at the corners of her eyes.

There had been a glow in her heart the minute she rose this morning. Shandra knew it was Grandmother telling her she'd made the right choice. "She's with us."

Aunt Jo peered into her eyes and smiled. "And you would know." She placed a single eagle feather in Shandra's hair. "This signifies you are single. After the ceremony we will place a second feather in your hair, showing you are married."

Wendy peeked out of the teepee. "They are ready."

The women each gave Shandra a hug and exited. The drum boomed twice.

She exited the teepee at the same time as Ryan. He grinned and raised an eyebrow.

The soft moccasins and leggings Aunt Jo had given her to wear, cushioned her steps as she walked to Ryan. He grasped her hand and led her over to Aunt Velma and a minister from the church in Nespelem. Shandra had been thankful that Ryan didn't care if he were married by a Catholic priest or not. He believed in their personal vows more than he did the sacred vows of a church.

Their immediate family members stood on either side of Velma and the minister facing Shandra and Ryan.

Velma said something in Nez Perce then repeated it in English. It was the Lord's Prayer. She continued to speak of the togetherness of nature and how so many animals get along while living in close proximity to one another and how we as people should learn from their co-existence.

The minister cleared his throat and read the

scripture from 1 Corinthians 13:4-8. When he finished he extended his hand to Shandra. "I believe you have written your own vows."

She nodded and cleared her throat. Holding Ryan's hands and gazing into his eyes, she began, "Like the new born filly struggling to stand on her own, I struggled with who I was and how to stand on my own. I had finally found my legs after an experience that had left me wondering why? The day you walked into the art gallery, I felt your compassion, your strength, and your belief in me. Your belief in my heritage and who I am. For that I give you my strength, my faith, my love."

She saw tears glittering in his eyes.

He raised her hands to his lips and kissed her knuckles.

Ryan cleared his throat and smiled at the best thing that had ever happened to him. "Shandra, from the moment I set eyes on you, I knew you were a strong, caring woman. Each moment I spend with you only increases my desire to be by your side for the rest of your life. You taking this step makes me believe we can live long and enjoy life together. I will never do anything to make you doubt my love, my trust, or my honor." He turned sideways and reached out with one hand. Andy placed the lead rope to the colt he'd purchased into his hand. "I not only give you my heart, I give you your heritage."

Shandra's eyes widened as she studied the horse. "He's beautiful! How? When?" She took the rope, ran her hands down the horse's neck and looked him all over before handing the lead rope back to Andy. He led the horse over to the side.

"I picked him out right after he was born," Ryan

captured her hands again and peered into her eyes. The emotions swimming in her eyes made his heart swell.

The minister said words about the circle of life and held out their rings.

Ryan watched as Shandra put the ring she wouldn't let him see on his finger. It was a small silver band with an engraved feather.

He picked up the silver and turquoise ring he'd had made by a silversmith. She inhaled as he placed it on her finger.

"It's beautiful!" she exclaimed.

Velma stepped forward with a star quilt. She placed it around their shoulders, holding them together. She said some words he didn't understand but it didn't matter as he found Shandra's hand and held on.

"I now pronounce you man and wife. You may kiss your bride," the minister said.

Ryan pulled Shandra into his arms and kissed her.

~*~

"Traditionally, our family would have given Ryan's family gifts and Ryan's family would have given us gifts. But I think the two of you finding one another is enough gift for all of us," Aunt Jo said, smiling at Shandra and grasping Ryan's hand after everyone had filled their plates with salmon and other delicious food. "Welcome to the family."

"Thank you. You've all made me feel a part of the family since I first met you," Ryan said, putting his arm around Shandra's shoulders.

The whole event felt like a big happy dream. However, Ryan holding onto her and seeing the Higheagle and Greer happy faces, she knew it was real.

"My only question is, you told me to take a week

off from work for the honeymoon, and you'd tell us where we were going," Ryan said, giving her aunt his best interrogation stare.

Uncle Martin held out a brochure. "A distant cousin of mine has a hunting lodge in the Wallowa Mountains. This time of year, it's mainly backpackers and the like who wander through there. I thought you two could use a vacation away from everything."

Shandra read the brochure. *Charlie's Hunting Lodge in the heart of the Wallowa Mountains. The only way in is by horse or air.*

"This sounds very remote." She glanced over her shoulder at Ryan. "What do you think?"

"If it's some place work can't call me and you aren't heckled by gallery owners, then I'm packed and ready to go," Ryan grabbed the brochure and started reading.

Shandra shrugged. "I guess we're headed to Charlie's Hunting Lodge."

Thank you for reading ***Dangerous Dance***. I enjoyed taking Shandra and Ryan back to the Colville Reservation and visiting with her family again. Researching the Seven Drum religion and figuring out how to make their marriage memorable for you, the reader, was not only challenging but fun. I hope you will continue to follow Shandra and Ryan's investigations as they now work together to solve murders as a married couple.

Be on the lookout for my new series releasing in January. The first Gabriel Hawke Mystery book is titled ***Murder of Ravens***.

If you enjoyed this book, please leave a review. It is the best way to thank an author for an enjoyable read. I love to hear from fans. You can contact me through my website, www.patyjager.net.

All my work has Western or Native American elements in them along with hints of humor and engaging characters. My husband and I raise alfalfa hay in rural eastern Oregon. Riding horses and battling rattlesnakes, I not only write the western lifestyle, I live it.

Paty

Windtree
Press

Thank you for purchasing this Windtree Press publication.
For other books of the heart, please visit our website
at www.windtreepress.com.

For questions or more information contact us
at info@windtreepress.com.

Windtree Press
www.windtreepress.com

Hillsboro, OR 97124

www.ingramcontent.com/pod-product-compliance
Lightning Source LLC
Chambersburg PA
CBHW070940190726
48292CB00004B/1275